in said. "I wish you could have heard everyone raving about it after you left rehearsal last night."

"Thanks," Chrissy said shyly.

Reaching across the table, Robin covered her hand with his own. Chrissy felt as though he'd started a fire that traveled up her arm all the way to her heart. "I was hoping we could work something out. We'd like to do some of your songs at the Heart-throb Hop. You're coming to rehearsal tomorrow night?"

"Definitely," Chrissy answered.

"Good." Robin stood up. "I'll see you then." Suddenly he bent down and gave her a quick kiss on the cheek. "I can't believe I met you, Chrissy McCall. I must be doing something right to deserve this kind of a lucky break." Then he strode off, the heels of his black cowboy boots making a clicking noise on the red tile floor.

Chrissy leaned back in her chair and took a slow sip of her drink. She wasn't just going to the dance with the band, she was going to sing with them! And not just one song, either!

On top of all that, Robin had kissed her— even if it was only on the cheek. Everything was falling into place. Her music career, her love life . . . everything!

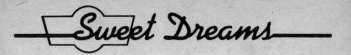

ROCK 'N' ROLL SWEETHEART

Laurie Lykken

BANTAM BOOKS
NEW YORK · TORONTO · LONDON · SYDNEY · AUCKLAND

RL 6, IL age 11 and up

ROCK 'N' ROLL SWEETHEART
A Bantam Book / April 1990

*Sweet Dreams and its associated logo are registered trademarks of
Bantam Books, a division of Bantam Doubleday Dell Publishing
Group, Inc. Registered in U.S. Patent and Trademark Office
and elsewhere.*

Cover photo by Pat Hill

All rights reserved.
Copyright © 1990 by Cloverdale Press Inc.
*No part of this book may be reproduced or transmitted
in any form or by any means, electronic or mechanical,
including photocopying, recording, or by any information
storage and retrieval system, without permission in
writing from the publisher.*
For information address: Bantam Books.

ISBN 0-553-28383-9

Published simultaneously in the United States and Canada

*Bantam Books are published by Bantam Books, a division of Bantam
Doubleday Dell Publishing Group, Inc. Its trademark, consisting of the
words "Bantam Books" and the portrayal of a rooster, is Registered in
U.S. Patent and Trademark Office and in other countries. Marca
Registrada. Bantam Books, 666 Fifth Avenue, New York, New York
10103.*

PRINTED IN THE UNITED STATES OF AMERICA

OPM   0   9   8   7   6   5   4   3   2   1

For Heather Duggan—an aspiring author.

Chapter One

Chrissy McCall breezed into the kitchen, humming her favorite song, Angelina's current pop single, "I'm Your Girl." Pausing by the sink, she smiled at the cozy scene her parents made sitting side by side at the kitchen table, sharing the newspaper.

"Good morning!" she said cheerfully as she switched off her cassette player and slipped the headphones down around her neck.

"Hi, honey." Mrs. McCall looked up and smiled at Chrissy, then folded the newspaper and set it down on the table. "Grab a bowl. We're having cereal this morning."

Mr. McCall lowered the sports section enough to peer over the top of it. "Well, since you've unplugged yourself, I guess that means no more reading the paper for me."

Chrissy grabbed a bowl from the cupboard

and sat down at the table with them. "That was the deal we made, Dad," Chrissy said, waving her spoon at him. "But I'm willing to forget it if you are."

"Forgoing the sports section to talk with my only child is definitely a tall order, but I can handle it," Chrissy's father said with a wry chuckle.

Chrissy groaned. "Please, Dad! No tall jokes or I'll plug myself back in, deal or no deal!"

"Tall jokes? What did I say?" Mr. McCall asked. He stood up and headed for the coffee maker on the counter. "Can you tell me what I said, Sarah?"

"Oh, Chrissy," her mother said, reaching across the table to smooth Chrissy's dark-brown bangs back from her forehead. "You're not going to start complaining about being tall again, are you?"

Chrissy reached for a box of cereal and began shaking some into her bowl. "Since I can't do anything about it, I should at least be able to complain now and then." She patted her tape player. "Angelina's only five foot four, you know."

"Really?" Mr. McCall took a sip of the coffee he had just poured for himself. "That's funny. She sings like she's much *taller* than that."

"Dad!" Chrissy cried.

"Now, Evan," Mrs. McCall cautioned him. "Don't tease."

"Anyway, you know that that's not what I meant, Dad. Being small like Angelina is romantic. Guys like girls who are tiny and delicate. No one's probably ever going to take me seriously as a singer/songwriter because of my height. I'm doomed before I've even gotten started. It's hard not to complain about that."

"I'm sorry," Mr. McCall apologized. "It's just that I've always been glad I'm tall." He straightened up to his full six feet six inches, stuck out his chest, and strutted around the room to demonstrate.

Chrissy's mother laughed so hard there were tears in her eyes. "Please, Evan. You're going to make my mascara run if you keep this up, and I don't have time to fix it."

"Yeah, Dad. You're being silly," Chrissy told him, trying her hardest not to laugh herself. "Of course you're glad to be tall. You're a guy. It's different for a girl."

Chrissy's father frowned. "That's kind of a sexist remark, isn't it, honey?" he asked. "And anyway, look at your mother. She's tall, and it hasn't hurt her any."

Chrissy turned and looked at her mother. At just under five foot nine, Sarah McCall, now in her late thirties, looked slim and attractive, with dark hair and eyes just like Chrissy's. She was obviously completely at ease with her above-average height. Of course, having a husband who was tall enough to tower over her didn't hurt. In fact, next to Evan McCall, Chrissy's mother looked almost petite.

"But I'm not just tall like Mom, I'm *too* tall," Chrissy insisted.

Mr. McCall's eyebrows drew together in a perplexed scowl. "How can a person be *too* tall?"

"I think Chrissy means she's too tall for the boys at school," her mother said, giving her daughter a gentle look.

"Any boy who can't see what a beautiful girl you are isn't worth much anyway," her father declared.

Ignoring her husband's outburst, Chrissy's mother said, "I know I've told you this before, honey, but I'll tell you again. I used to feel the same way you do now. I thought I'd never find the right boy. But boys just grow up a little more slowly. They'll catch up one day, though. And when they do . . ."

"Sarah," Mr. McCall protested, "you make it sound like boys are—"

"Let's change the subject, okay?" Chrissy suggested, interrupting her father. "Anyway, it's almost time for me to go."

Mrs. McCall glanced at the kitchen clock. "You're right. I've got to be on my way, too. I've got a long day ahead of me." She took another sip of coffee, then stood up. "My first client is coming in at nine o'clock. I can't tell you how

4

much I'm looking forward to next week! I might even be able to start coming home at four again."

"You mean, you're not coming home at four today?" Chrissy asked. "Then who's giving me a ride to work?"

"Not me," her father told her as he wiped his hands on a dish towel. "I've got customers coming down from Minneapolis late this afternoon. I'll probably be tied up with them until at least eight o'clock."

"Oh, Evan!" Mrs. McCall said with a sigh. "I thought we had settled all this. I can't possibly leave work early today."

Chrissy gathered up her books and started backing toward the kitchen door. "Don't worry about it, you guys. There's always the city bus." She thought of the snowy bus stop and shivered. If she had known that her parents were too busy to drive her to work after school, she would never have put on her denim miniskirt. But it was too late to change now. The school bus would be at the bottom of the McCalls' driveway in just a few minutes.

Chrissy's father shook his head as he slipped on his suit coat and then his wool overcoat. "How about Duncan? Maybe if we call the Wests right now, we can still catch him before he leaves for school."

Chrissy had to bite her tongue to keep from complaining. It seemed as if her parents and the Wests were always trying to bring Duncan and her together. Since they were best friends, they thought Duncan and Chrissy ought to be, too.

"Good idea, Evan," Mrs. McCall said, bustling past Chrissy into the front hall. "I'll call Elinore from my office and set it up."

Chrissy shook her head. "I'll just find Duncan at school, Mom. Our paths usually cross at least once during the day." She pulled her down parka out of the front closet. She had planned on wearing her short pink wool coat, but if she was going to end up taking the bus across town to her job at the Edmond Heights Mall, the parka would be warmer. She gave her mother a quick kiss on the cheek. "I'll get there somehow. Don't worry about me."

"That's our girl. I'll be at the mall at nine to pick you up as usual," her father assured her, joining them in the front hall. "I'll even take you out for ice cream or pie afterward to make it up to you."

Chrissy grinned. "All right! We haven't been out for dessert together for ages."

"Can I come, too?" Mrs. McCall asked.

"Well . . ." Mr. McCall winked at Chrissy as he pretended to consider, then slipped his arm around his wife's waist and gave her a squeeze. "Of course, my dear. We'll make it a family celebration."

Just then there was a loud honk. "Oh, my gosh! There's the bus!" Chrissy cried, flinging open the door. "Bye!" she called back over her shoulder.

Chrissy practically skated down the driveway in her black flats. "Sorry," she told the bus driver breathlessly as she quickly scaled the steps. Then, spotting her best friend Beth Knight's blond, curly hair near the middle of the bus, Chrissy waved and hurried to join her.

"I was afraid you were sick or something," Beth said, sliding closer to the window to make room for Chrissy. "I was afraid I'd burst if I had to wait another minute to tell you who called me last night."

"Let me guess." Chrissy leaned back and closed her eyes. "Let's see. Was it . . . Paul Brady?"

Beth sighed dreamily. "Don't I wish! But no such luck. It was Avis Anderson. She's going to the dance with Mike Rouner!"

"You mean the Heartthrob Hop?" Chrissy asked, and Beth nodded. "I thought she was going with us!" Chrissy cried.

"Come on, Chrissy. If a guy that you'd been dying to go out with asked you to the Heart-throb Hop, wouldn't *you* go?"

Chrissy shook her head. "Not if I'd made other plans with my friends first."

"Well, I told her that we'd *all* do the same thing if we had a chance. She said she was afraid you'd be mad at her, but I told her you wouldn't be," Beth said.

"Well, I am," Chrissy insisted. "I'd never cancel out of plans I'd already made with a friend like that. You wouldn't either."

"I'm not so sure," Beth said thoughtfully. "Oh, well. I doubt anyone will ask me anyway. You and Vicky and I will go together," Beth assured her, but she didn't sound very happy about the idea. "We don't need Avis to have fun anyway."

Chrissy giggled. "You know, that could be a song! Here, give me something to write with." Beth quickly dug into her oversize canvas bag and produced a pencil, which she handed to Chrissy.

"Who needs you anyway?" Chrissy said in a singsong voice as she wrote the words on the back of her biology notebook. "First you say you will, then you won't. Then you say you can, but you don't."

Beth laughed as she read the beginnings of Chrissy's latest song over her shoulder. "I don't really think accepting a date with Michael Rouner was as treacherous as all that, do you?"

Chrissy tapped the pencil on her notebook. "I guess not. It's just that I really want to hear Robin and the Hoods play, and I can't go to the Heartthrob Hop alone." Just the thought of standing on the sidelines by herself at the school's winter dance made Chrissy shudder. For the second time that day, Chrissy found herself thinking that her height was a curse. Everyone would notice her standing alone at the dance, because she was so tall.

The bus pulled to a stop, and Chrissy and Beth got off and headed up the steps into the high school. They were crossing the main foyer when a male voice shouted, "Hi, Beth!" loud enough to rise above the dull roar of the crowd.

Beth's blue eyes widened. "It's Paul Brady," she whispered excitedly. She gave Chrissy a poke with her elbow. Then, putting on a big smile as she waved, Beth called back, "Hi, Paul!"

When they finally reached Beth's locker a few minutes later, Beth turned toward Chrissy. "Do you believe it! I mean, he really went out of his way to say hi, didn't he?"

Chrissy nodded. "He seems to really like you." She wanted to be happy for Beth, but if Beth ended up going to the Heartthrob Hop with Paul, where would that leave Chrissy? She knew that their other friend, Vicky Nord, had been trying to get her neighbor, Dave Mullen, to ask her to the Hop. If Dave asked Vicky, Chrissy wasn't going to be able to hear her favorite local band perform. There was no way she was going to the dance alone.

"Uh-oh," Chrissy said, suddenly spotting a

familiar black fedora hat at the far end of the hall. "There's Duncan."

Beth giggled. "Want me to hide you?"

Chrissy laughed. "Not this time. Thanks to my parents, I have to ask him for a ride to work this afternoon. I'll see you at lunch, okay?"

"Sure," Beth said. "Bye."

Tightening her grip on her books, Chrissy began weaving her way through the congested hallway. At the moment, being tall was a definite advantage. If she had been any shorter, she would never have been able to keep her eyes on Duncan's trademark hat as he moved off down the hall.

Duncan wiggled his eyebrows at her when she finally caught up with him. "Hey, Chrissy," he said. "Forget something this morning? Like your jeans?" He lifted the camera that was always hanging around his neck and started focusing it.

Chrissy looked down at her bare legs and realized that her miniskirt was completely hidden by her big down parka. She felt her cheeks get hot. "I'm wearing a skirt," she said. "But go ahead and take a picture and embarrass me if it makes you happy."

"Lighten up," he told her, lowering his camera. "Can't you take a joke?"

"I could if it were funny," Chrissy retorted. It was times like this that made her think she'd have nothing to do with Duncan if his parents weren't her parents' best friends.

"Okay. So what's up?" he asked.

"I need a favor," she said. "Do you think you could give me a ride to the mall after school today?"

"Today," Duncan repeated thoughtfully. He pushed his fedora back on his sandy-haired head and looked up at the ceiling. Then he slowly lowered his eyes again. "I think that might be possible. Of course, you'll have to ride in the Green Pea."

Chrissy nodded. "I know." The Green Pea was the nickname Duncan's ten-year-old sister, Annie, had given his beat-up, secondhand car.

"And you can't make fun of her," Duncan insisted.

"I won't," Chrissy promised.

"Then meet me by the trophy case outside the gym right after school." He looked back down at Chrissy's bare legs. "Nice legs," he said. "Maybe I really should take a quick picture of them for the *Buzzette*. Maybe I could take pictures of a whole bunch of legs and start a contest to see who could match the top halves of certain people with the bottom halves." Duncan winked at Chrissy. "What do you think?"

Chrissy laughed in spite of herself. "I think you're crazy," she told him. Then she spun around and headed back in the direction she had come as quickly as she could, before Duncan had the chance to decide that his idea was a good one after all.

If she stopped, Duncan would probably take her picture. He was always doing that, usually when she least expected it. She was never sure where or when one of Duncan's notorious candid pictures would show up in print, either. He seemed to get his crazy pictures published everywhere, from the school *Buzzette* to the town's local biweekly paper, the Edmond Heights *Sentinel*. About the only certainty where Duncan West was concerned was that whenever one of his many pictures of Chrissy appeared, it was horribly embarrassing.

"Don't forget!" Duncan called after her. "The trophy case right after school."

"I'll be there!" Chrissy said over her shoulder with a sigh.

Chapter Two

When the bell signaling the end of the school day rang, Chrissy dashed out of her English class and hurried toward her locker. Quickly, she dialed her combination, grabbed her stuff, and headed downstairs.

Too late, Chrissy remembered that the trophy case where Duncan had asked her to meet him was on the other side of the gym. But luckily the gym doors were open, so she could cut across the gym to the other side.

She heard shouting just as she was about to go into the gym. Then she heard the pounding and squeaking of sneakers thundering across the wooden floor in her direction.

Standing in the doorway, she peered cautiously into the gym, where several senior boys were playing basketball. She spotted Duncan's familiar fedora through the open doors on the other side of the gym. He was already by the trophy case, waiting for her. Somehow, she had to get across the gym, despite the basketball game. If she didn't, she risked losing her ride. Duncan wasn't the most patient person in the world.

Taking a deep breath, Chrissy slipped into the gym and prayed that the boys wouldn't look up and notice her. Slowly she edged along the wall toward the back of the bleachers.

"Over here!" one of the boys yelled. Then they all thundered in another direction.

Quickly, Chrissy ducked underneath the metal bleachers. Crouched down, she had nearly gotten halfway across when she felt the collar of her pullover snag on something. She reached up and did her best to untangle it from the bleacher. But try as she might, she couldn't get the little bit of pinched wool loose. If she forced it, she would ruin her favorite sweater. But if she didn't get out of there right away, she was going to miss her ride to work!

Feeling she had no choice, Chrissy cried, "Help!" as loudly as she could. Then she waited for a second before yelling "Help!" again. Chrissy heard the running on the court stop after her second yell.

"It's coming from under the bleachers," she heard one of the boys say.

"You're right," another boy said. A minute

later, ten anxious faces were peering at Chrissy from the end of the bleachers.

"Hi," she said sheepishly.

"Hi," a tall, redheaded boy said. "Is something wrong?"

Chrissy cleared her throat. "I'm, uh, stuck under here."

The boys looked at each other, then the redhead ducked down and began edging toward her. Chrissy noticed right away that he was nearly as tall as her father. She smiled. Maybe getting stuck like this wasn't going to be awful, after all.

"How are you stuck?" the boy asked when he'd finally reached her.

Chrissy bent her head down even farther and did the best she could to point at the collar of her sweater. He reached up and unhooked the snag, his fingers accidentally grazing the sensitive skin on the back of her neck. Chrissy felt little bumps of gooseflesh form on her arms. "There, you're free," he declared.

"Thanks," Chrissy told him. He looked just as embarrassed as she felt. But he smiled and nodded his head like a hero in an old western movie.

"Anytime," he said. Then he cried, "Ouch!" as his head hit one of the metal support bars.

"Be careful," Chrissy warned, stifling a giggle. "It's dangerous for tall people under here."

He grinned down at her. "What were you doing under the bleachers, anyway?" he asked, rubbing the back of his head as he and Chrissy crept out from behind them.

Before Chrissy could explain, however, there was a blinding flash of light.

"Gotcha!" Duncan declared delightedly. He lowered his camera and grinned triumphantly at her.

"Duncan West!" Chrissy yelled. "Give me that camera!"

Duncan chuckled. "Fat chance, McCall."

Chrissy was so mad, she was barely aware of the basketball players who had formed an amused semicircle behind Duncan.

"I'm going to kill you," she muttered fiercely, moving closer to Duncan. "And this time I mean it!" She held out her hands menacingly.

Chrissy heard a chorus of male laughter, and she remembered the redhead who had been kind enough to help her. She turned around to apologize for getting him into this mess, but he had vanished.

Leading Duncan across the gym, she demanded, "Why do you do things like this to me?"

Duncan shrugged. "Can I help it if you're always getting yourself into ridiculous situations that demand to be captured on film? Besides, Jeff Henderson is big news around Edmond High these days. He's the star of the basketball team—a basketball team that could very possibly win the state championship."

"I don't keep track of all that stuff," Chrissy said defensively. She'd really been too busy with her job and homework and music to keep track of the sports scene at school. Basketball had never been one of her favorite sports anyway. She'd had too many people suggest that she take up the game herself just because she was so tall.

"Just think of the great caption that could go under that picture if it turns out," Duncan mused. " 'Basketball star schedules private practice' or maybe—"

Chrissy held up her hands. "Please, enough already! I think I get the idea." Then, taking hold of the sleeve of Duncan's brown leather bomber jacket, Chrissy began pulling him out of the gym. "If I didn't need a ride to work, I'd tell you to get lost," she mumbled, letting go of his sleeve once they were safely headed outside. "That guy was just trying to help me get my sweater loose. There's absolutely nothing going on between us."

"That's not how it looked from where I stood," Duncan pointed out. "Anyway, you should be happy."

"Happy! Because you're going to use a picture to embarrass me in front of the entire school?"

17

"Come on, Chrissy. Lighten up. It was a funny scene that made a funny picture—if it even turns out! To tell you the truth, I'm not sure I got my camera in focus. It could all just be a blur. Anyway, where's your sense of humor?"

"Duncan West, if that picture appears in the *Buzzette* this week, you'd better hire a bodyguard," Chrissy threatened, stopping by the Green Pea.

Duncan unlocked the passenger door of the car and opened it for Chrissy. "Don't worry, I wasn't planning on using the picture in the school paper."

"Really?" Chrissy asked suspiciously.

"Really," he assured her.

Chrissy sighed with relief. "Well, thanks for that anyway."

"Hey, you're not still mad, are you?" Duncan asked as the Green Pea coughed a couple of times before finally starting.

Chrissy stared at him. "Oh, no. Why would I be mad? I love looking like a fool in front of a bunch of senior boys. It's just what every junior girl wants."

"I suppose you have a point," Duncan admitted. He backed out of the parking space and drove slowly out of the school parking lot. Then he smiled. "Say, I've got a great idea. How about calling in sick and going skating with me this afternoon instead of working? That way I can make all this up to you. You know, show you how sorry I am. I'll even make you a cup of my famous hot chocolate afterward. How about it? It'll be just like old times."

Chrissy shook her head even though she loved skating. "I can't. I really like my job at The Golden Note. I've almost got enough money saved up to buy the electric guitar and amp I told you about, but I'll need my store discount to do it. I don't want to blow it now."

"I can understand that," Duncan agreed, but he sounded wistful. "It was just a thought."

Chrissy smiled. "I might consider skating with you another time, though."

Duncan drove into the mall parking lot a minute later and pulled to a stop right by the entrance. "Really?" He lifted his black fedora and raked his sandy-brown hair back with his fingers. Then he replaced his hat and gave Chrissy a thoughtful look.

Chrissy nodded. "Really. On one condition. You have to promise to give me a certain negative." She'd known Duncan long enough not to trust him. As long as he had the negative of the picture of Jeff and her, there was a chance it would get printed somewhere.

"That's blackmail!" Duncan chided her.

"Look, if you go around taking pictures of people without asking permission first"—Chrissy shook her finger at him—"you *deserve* to be blackmailed!" With that, she hopped out of Duncan's car. Biting her tongue to keep from laughing, she hurried toward the mall.

"You're welcome!" she heard Duncan call after her. Then she heard the Green Pea roar off. Duncan definitely needed a new muffler for his car. Chrissy half-hoped he would get a ticket for disturbing the peace.

Yanking open the glass door, Chrissy stepped inside the mall. One day Duncan West was going to drive her totally nuts. One second he could be perfectly sweet and nice, and the next second he'd be an outrageous tease again. She was positive that Jeff Henderson had disappeared because he had been embarrassed by Duncan's picture-taking. Chrissy shook her head. Jeff was actually kind of cute, and he was tall, too. Maybe . . . but no. Chrissy didn't stand a chance with Jeff now. Duncan had seen to that.

When Chrissy entered The Golden Note, her mind was still on the disaster in the gym. She had always wanted to be famous, but she had wanted to be famous for her music, not for a bunch of silly pictures. She headed for the back room, where she hung up her parka and slipped the regulation yellow smock over her clothes.

"Hi, Chrissy," Mr. Levi, the store manager, said when Chrissy came back out on the sales floor. "You're early today."

"Does that mean I get a longer break for dinner?" she asked hopefully.

"I'm afraid not. Elton just called in sick. It's just going to be the two of us tonight unless I can get hold of Becky. I'm going to try her now. Can you keep an eye on things out here?"

Chrissy nodded. "No problem."

As soon as Mr. Levi ducked into the back room, Chrissy picked up the electric guitar she had been coveting for over a year. It was a hot-pink Fender with a sleek, black neck. Four more paychecks, she told herself, and it was hers!

The store was empty, as it often was early in the afternoon. Pretty soon, the after-school crowd would hit the mall, and they'd be swamped with browsers. But for now, Chrissy could afford to fool around a bit.

She plugged the guitar into an amp, being careful to keep the volume low. Then, closing her eyes, she began strumming a tentative tune to go along with the lyrics she had written on the bus that morning.

"Hey, great tune. Sounds like one of Angelina's songs. Am I right?"

Chrissy stopped playing. "It's . . ." she began, looking up, prepared to smile at her unexpected audience. But instead of smiling, she gasped. Robin James, the lead singer of her favorite local band, Robin and the Hoods, was standing right in front of her, his hands stuffed into the pockets of his silver-studded black leather jacket. "Robin James!" Chrissy cried.

"Hi," he said, obviously pleased that Chrissy had recognized him. "Do I know you?"

"No. I mean, I don't think so. But I know you. I've heard your band, and I really love your music," Chrissy said all in a rush. Robin had graduated from Edmond High the year before, but she hadn't really noticed him much at school. He and his friends hadn't started their band until a year ago, but they were already incredibly popular.

Robin smiled as he leaned across the counter that separated them. Even smiling, he was tough looking, Chrissy decided. His spiked, close-cropped hair was the same shiny black as his leather jacket, and his eyes were a cool steel-gray. He even had a small silver stud in his right ear. "Thanks. You're pretty good on that guitar. Have you been playing long?" he asked.

"Practically since I could sit up," Chrissy said proudly. Then she patted the guitar. "This is going to be mine soon. Right now I'm still acoustic."

"So, was that a new Angelina song, Chrissy?" Robin asked again. "I haven't heard everything on her latest album."

"Actually, it's one of my own songs," Chrissy told him, a little surprised that Robin knew her name. Then she remembered the name tag pinned to her yellow smock. She touched it

22

self-consciously and laughed. "But you're right about its being new. It's so new, in fact, it isn't even finished yet. I just started writing it today. Does it really sound like something Angelina's done? I wouldn't copy anything of hers on purpose, you know. She's one of my favorites, though. Maybe I listen to her too much."

"You mean you wrote that song yourself?" he demanded. When Chrissy nodded, Robin whistled appreciatively. "It's good enough to be one of hers." He looked at Chrissy thoughtfully for a moment, then added, "That could be a big hit. The right people would have to hear it, of course. I guess that's the biggest trick in the music business, just getting heard by the right people."

"Do you really think it's good?" Chrissy asked eagerly. She set the electric guitar back in its soft, velvet-lined case. She wanted to pinch herself to make sure she wasn't dreaming, but she was afraid if she did, she'd wake herself up. And this was a dream she didn't want to end!

"It's got definite possibilities. I'd like to hear it when it's done. Maybe you could come to one of the band's rehearsals sometime and play it for us."

"Sure," Chrissy said enthusiastically. "That would be great."

"You could bring your guitar with you," he added, nodding at the case.

Chrissy sighed. "That's not mine, remember?

I'm working on it, though. And I'm getting real close." She tugged nervously on her yellow smock.

"Bring your old guitar then." He took a leather wallet out of his back pocket and pulled out a business card. "Here's where we rehearse," he told her, tapping the address on the card. "It's the basement of my parents' house. They had it soundproofed for us. Anyway, me and the guys are there most nights until midnight at least. Stop over anytime."

"Oh, I will," she said.

Robin laughed. "I feel like I should say good-bye now, but actually, I came in for some guitar strings. I need the double-wound kind, heavy gauge."

Chrissy hurried out from behind the counter. "Hang on, I'll get a set for you."

"Make that three sets!" he called after her.

"How's it going?" Mr. Levi asked as Chrissy darted into the back room for a new box of guitar strings.

"Fine," Chrissy assured her boss. "There's only been one customer so far." She waved the packages of strings she'd taken out of the box at Mr. Levi. "He needs these."

"I've got good news. I got hold of Becky and she'll be here in half an hour. Looks like you won't starve after all," he teased.

"Thanks," Chrissy said, then she hurried back to Robin.

"Here you go," she told him, pulling a set out of the box. "Are these what you wanted?"

"Exactly what I had in mind," he said, taking one of the strings out of its package and examining it.

Chrissy quickly rang up the sale. As Robin handed Chrissy the money, he said, "Guess I'll be seeing you as soon as you get that song finished. Right?"

"I have others, too," Chrissy told him. "In fact, I have lots more."

"Bring them. We're looking for some fresh material. Maybe we can work out a deal if one or two of them sound right for us." He gave her a little salute, then turned and left the store, his black boots clicking across the floor.

When he was gone, Chrissy began to wonder if she hadn't just imagined the whole thing. But then she saw she was still holding Robin's card. "Robin and the Hoods," it said along the top, and below it was an address and a phone number. *This,* she told herself, *might just be my big break!*

Chapter Three

"Beth!" Chrissy called, waving wildly when she spotted her best friend in the lunch line. Beth returned Chrissy's wave and headed over to the table where Chrissy was sitting with Avis and Vicky.

"Hi, all," Beth said cheerfully.

"We thought you were sick," Avis said, shaking a carrot stick at Beth.

"You did? Why?" Beth asked. She slid her lunch tray between Vicky and Chrissy and sat down.

Chrissy shrugged. "You weren't on the bus this morning."

Beth smiled mysteriously. "I got a ride," she said.

Chrissy lifted her eyebrows. "Oh? How come?"

Beth's smile widened. "Wrong question. You're supposed to ask, who with?"

All three girls leaned closer to Beth. "Well?" Chrissy asked.

"I'll give you a hint. His initials are PSB." Beth winked at Chrissy.

Avis tugged thoughtfully on her silver hoop earring. "Isn't that the initials of the educational TV channel?"

Beth giggled. "No, that's PBS. I said PSB, and those are Paul Brady's initials. His middle name is Stephen," she added.

"Paul drove you to school!" Chrissy cried.

"Shhh," Beth said, looking around nervously.

"Don't worry, Beth. No one's listening to us," Vicky assured her.

"Still," Beth cautioned.

"Paul called you, and you didn't tell me?" Chrissy asked, astonished.

"He called last night. You were at work," Beth reminded her. "I did try calling around ten, but no one was home at your house. I would have tried again later, but your parents have that rule about not calling after ten."

Chrissy nodded. "They're pretty strict about that, too."

"Where were you, anyway?" Beth asked.

"My parents took me out for dessert after work," Chrissy told her. "It was nice."

"So tell us, Beth," Avis urged. "What happened?"

"Paul invited me to go to the Heartthrob Hop with him!" Beth said.

"All right!" Vicky cried.

"It's about time," Avis muttered, shaking her head.

"That's great, Beth," Chrissy told her.

"Do you really mean it?" Beth asked Chrissy. "You aren't mad?"

Chrissy shook her head. "No. I sort of thought this would happen."

"I *knew* it would happen," Avis said. "Maybe we can even double, Beth. I'll talk to Michael about it this afternoon."

"Now, if Dave would only call me," Vicky said wistfully.

"Isn't Dave a friend of Paul's?" Avis asked. "Maybe you could ask him to suggest to Dave that he call Vicky about the dance. Then we could triple!"

"*Could* you ask Paul about it, Beth?" Vicky pleaded. "Dave's the kind of guy who needs coaching."

Beth laughed. "Sure, Vicky. I'll do what I can. And you come with us, too, Chrissy. Okay? I mean, there'll be so many of us, it won't really matter if you don't have a date."

Chrissy shrugged. "I'll think about it," she said.

Later, after Vicky and Avis had left, Beth turned to Chrissy and said, "I know how you feel about friends backing out of plans with other friends just because a boy happens to call. But I really meant what I said about you com-

29

ing along with us. Maybe we can even fix you up with someone."

"Maybe I won't need a blind date," Chrissy told her mysteriously.

"What does that mean?" Beth asked eagerly. "Has something happened that I don't know about?"

"It means I've got some news of my own." Chrissy smiled at the memory of talking to Robin at the music store.

"You do! Why didn't you say something earlier?" Beth demanded. "Has someone asked you to the dance, too? Who?"

"It's better than that. But you've got to promise not to say anything to anyone just in case it doesn't work out. That's why I didn't want to say anything while Vicky and Avis were here." Chrissy picked up her shoulder bag and carefully pulled Robin's calling card out of the zippered side pocket. She handed the card to Beth.

"Robin James gave it to me himself," Chrissy told her. "He came into The Golden Note yesterday to buy some guitar strings and heard me working on that song I started writing yesterday on the bus. He said he really liked the tune I was putting together and invited me to sit in on one of the band's rehearsals."

Beth's mouth dropped open. "Really? That's wonderful, Chrissy! It's just what you've always wanted, isn't it?"

Chrissy nodded. "It was so wonderful I was afraid I'd dreamed the whole thing. That card is the only thing I've got to convince myself that it actually happened."

"So are you going tonight?" Beth demanded. "What will you wear?"

"I'm definitely going, but I don't know what to wear," Chrissy confessed. "I've been too excited to think about it, and I was hoping you might help me decide. Could you come home with me this afternoon?"

"I would," Beth said, "but I'm catching a ride home with Paul. I could come over tomorrow, though."

"I have to go tonight," Chrissy said. "I have to work again tomorrow night, and I'm afraid if I don't go right away, Robin will forget that he even met me."

"You're probably right," Beth agreed. "You should go tonight, while your song is still fresh in his mind."

"Exactly what I thought. Should I call first? There's a phone number on the card." Chrissy slid her chair a little closer to Beth's. They were both looking down at Robin James's business card when a flash went off.

"Hi, girls," Duncan said a second later.

Chrissy snatched Robin's card out of Beth's hand and quickly slipped it into the pocket of her green wool vest.

"Hey," Beth said. "Where's your hat, Duncan?"

Duncan let out a big sigh. "Mr. Beckworth, our illustrious assistant principal, decided I couldn't wear my hat during class anymore. He said he's had complaints from more than one of my teachers about its being distracting."

"That doesn't surprise me," Chrissy told him. "What surprises me is that they let you wear that hat for five months without saying something sooner."

Duncan pointed at Chrissy with his thumb. "She's mad at me," he told Beth. "And just because I tried to immortalize her on film."

"Tried to humiliate me is more like it," Chrissy corrected him.

"Will one of you please tell me what you're talking about?" Beth asked.

Duncan pulled up a chair and sat down at the table. "You know who Jeff Henderson is, don't you?" he asked.

Beth nodded. "Of course. He's the center on the basketball team."

Duncan looked at Chrissy and clicked his tongue as he shook his head. "See, Chrissy? You're probably the only person at Edmond who doesn't know Jeff."

"I know him now," Chrissy pointed out. Then, turning to Beth, she explained, "Duncan tried to take an embarrassing picture of Jeff helping me unsnag my sweater under the bleachers last night."

"Under the bleachers?" Beth repeated.

"That's right," Duncan said. "Actually, the picture turned out a lot better than I thought it would."

"But you promised you wouldn't use it!" Chrissy cried.

"I only promised I wouldn't use it in the *Buzzette*. I never said I wouldn't give it to the *Echowan*," Duncan replied.

"You're going to put that picture in the year-book?" Now Chrissy really wanted to strangle him.

Duncan shrugged as he stood up. "I must admit, I'm thinking about it. It's just too good to toss out. Well, see you girls later."

"What were you doing under the bleachers with Jeff Henderson, anyway?" Beth asked as soon as Duncan was gone. "I mean, I didn't even know it was *possible* to get under the bleachers in the gym."

"It's a totally dumb story," Chrissy assured her.

"Well, at least the *Echowan* doesn't come out until the end of the year," Beth pointed out.

"Look, Beth," Chrissy said, taking Robin's card out of her vest pocket and putting it back into her shoulder bag, "promise me you won't say anything about Robin to Duncan."

"Do you really think Duncan would go to Robin's just to take your picture?" Beth looked amused.

"It isn't funny, at least not to me," Chrissy told her. "And please don't say anything to Avis or Vicky either." She stood up and picked up her tray.

"I just don't want to tell anyone in case it doesn't work out," she continued as she set her lunch tray on the conveyor belt. "You're the only person I really trust, Beth."

"I won't let you down," Beth assured her as they left the cafeteria. "You can count on me. After all, you are my best friend."

Beth took off for her locker where she was meeting Paul, and Chrissy slipped into the girls' bathroom to comb her hair. She still didn't know what she was going to wear to Robin's rehearsal. It had to be something spectacular— but not too obvious. She didn't want to look like some overly eager groupie.

Pulling a styling brush out of her shoulder bag, Chrissy joined the cluster of girls in front of the mirror. She had just finished brushing her long, dark-brown hair when she heard some girls from the cheerleading squad talking excitedly. Chrissy took out her blusher and began brushing her cheeks with it as she listened.

"Alex said Jeff was really embarrassed," Carolyn Lowe, the captain of the cheerleaders, said.

"I didn't even think anyone could *get* under the bleachers, much less someone as tall as Jeff," Sally Baker put in.

Chrissy felt her cheeks grow warm. Apparently they didn't realize that they were also talking about *her*!

"Why would anyone spy on the basketball team? I mean, why would a girl from our own school want to do that?" another girl demanded as Chrissy slowly backed toward the door.

"Who knows," Carolyn said, shaking her head. "Some girls just don't know how to get a boy's attention, I guess."

"Well, I think . . ." Sally began, but Chrissy didn't want to hear the rest of her comment. She slipped out the bathroom door and hurried down the hall.

She was about to go into her American history class when she saw Jeff standing just a few feet away. He was reading something on the bulletin board and didn't seem to notice her. Chrissy decided it was time to clear up the whole ridiculous incident once and for all.

"Hi," she said, walking boldly up to him.

Jeff looked up. When he saw Chrissy, he backed up a little. "Uh, hi," he mumbled.

"Look, I know what you think," she began, "but you're wrong. I wasn't spying on you guys, I was just trying to get to the other side of the gym without disturbing your game. I was meeting that guy with the camera. He's a friend of mine. Actually, his parents are friends of my parents. Know what I mean?"

Jeff narrowed his eyes suspiciously. "Who are you, anyway?" he asked.

"My name's Chrissy McCall," she told him, giving him a friendly smile. "I'm a junior." She couldn't help noticing how tall Jeff was. Suddenly, she realized she regretted the bleacher incident for more than one reason. But she could clearly see that it was too late to start over with Jeff. The best Chrissy could hope for was to put an end to the ridiculous rumors flying around Edmond High.

"Anyway," she went on, "the important thing is that you were nice enough to help me out. Thanks." She paused to smile at him. "And I've got some good news, too. Duncan isn't going to print that picture of us in the *Buzzette* because I was able to talk him out of it."

"The *Buzzette*?" Jeff repeated, looking even more nervous.

"Yeah, well, he does that two-page spread called Candid Clips every week." Chrissy had to admit that Duncan was good at catching kids doing funny things both on and off campus.

Jeff seemed to relax a little. Then, suddenly, there was a blinding flash of light. Chrissy jumped, and as she did, the stack of books she was holding slipped out of her arms.

"Ouch!" Jeff howled as Chrissy's heavy history book came crashing down on his right foot.

"Oh, my gosh! I'm sorry!" Chrissy bent down to pick up her book, and there was another flash of light. She straightened up and spun around. "Duncan West, you cut that out! Do you hear me?"

Duncan merely laughed and took off down the hall, just as the bell rang to start class.

She turned back toward Jeff, who was backing away, glaring at her. Chrissy shrugged. "What can I say? Like I told you, he's an old friend of the family's. I guess he thinks that makes him my personal photographer. Sorry!"

"Are you crazy? Stay away from me!" Jeff commanded just before he turned around and bolted.

Chrissy leaned back against the nearest locker and sighed. She could hardly blame Jeff for his reaction. Still, none of this was her fault. It was all so unfair. Duncan had always been a pest, but lately he'd gone too far.

Well, whatever Duncan was up to, Chrissy was more determined than ever that he know nothing about Robin James's interest in her music. The last thing she wanted was to have Duncan trail her to Robin's rehearsal. If he ruined that, she would never forgive him!

Chapter Four

"Can I use one of the cars tonight?" Chrissy asked as she got up to help her mother clear the dinner dishes from the table.

"Where are you headed?" Mr. McCall asked.

Chrissy crossed her fingers behind her back. She didn't like to lie to her parents, but she felt she had no choice. If they knew she was headed for Robin James's house to sit in on a band rehearsal, they might let something slip out about it to Duncan's parents. Once that happened, she'd never be able to keep her plans from Duncan.

"Beth asked me to come over," Chrissy said. "She wants to hear the new song I've been writing. She sort of inspired it on the bus. I was even thinking of calling it 'For Beth.' "

Mrs. McCall smiled. "I'd like to hear it sometime, too. What's it about?"

Chrissy thought for a moment. Then she said, "I guess it's about broken promises between friends."

"Mmm," her mother mused. "Sounds pretty serious."

Her father took his car keys out of his pants pocket and handed them to Chrissy. "You can take the Chevy. Be home by eleven. It's a school night, remember."

She nodded as she took the keys. "I know. Thanks."

Clutching the keys, she turned and hurried toward the stairs. Now she needed to find just the right outfit to wear to Robin's. As soon as she reached her room, Chrissy tossed the car keys into her shoulder bag. Then she turned toward her closet. What she really wanted to do was to go shopping, but there wasn't time for that. She was going to have to make do with something she already had.

There was her denim miniskirt, but she'd been wearing that at The Golden Note when Robin had invited her to his rehearsal. She didn't want him to think that was the only thing she owned. Her Aztec-print skirt caught her eye, but Chrissy knew instantly that it wouldn't do. Wearing a skirt was all wrong, she decided, heading for her dresser.

She yanked open her jeans drawer. The first pair she pulled out were covered with Mickey

Mouse patches. Chrissy wrinkled up her nose. Too young and silly, she told herself, tossing the jeans over her shoulder onto her bed. The next pair of jeans she pulled out were too nondescript. Chrissy didn't want Robin to think she was boring, so they went over her shoulder onto the bed as well. Finally she spotted her black jeans.

She hadn't worn them in such a long time that she'd even forgotten she owned them. Chrissy smiled as she remembered that everyone in the band wore black. The black jeans would be perfect! If she could only find her black tank top, she'd have the ideal outfit for a night with Robin and the Hoods.

Getting down on her hands and knees, Chrissy began pulling out all sorts of discarded items from the back of her closet, an area in her room her father referred to as "the black hole." She discovered all sorts of things she had completely forgotten about, including two skinny black leather belts with silver buckles that would go really well with her black jeans. She tossed the belts over her shoulder toward her bed.

"Ouch!" someone complained. Chrissy turned around and saw Duncan standing next to her bed, the belts lying at his feet.

"What are *you* doing?" she demanded.

"I might ask you the same question," he quipped.

Chrissy stood up and put her hands on her hips. "Well, you might have at least knocked," she said, glaring at him.

Duncan shrugged sheepishly. "Sorry. Your door was open. But I guess being Edmond High's candid photographer has given me a few bad habits."

"A few! That's an understatement if I ever heard one," Chrissy said, shaking her head.

"Look," Duncan said, "I really came over here to apologize, not to antagonize you more." He pushed the clothes spread all over Chrissy's bed out of the way and sat down.

"Apologize?" Chrissy repeated. "For what?"

"I suppose I could rattle off a lengthy list, but mostly I'm sorry I broke into whatever you were saying to Jeff Henderson this afternoon. I don't know what came over me. It wasn't even an interesting shot, to tell you the truth." Duncan pushed back his fedora and scratched his forehead thoughtfully.

Chrissy laughed. She'd forgotten all about Jeff. "Don't worry about it. He's kind of timid," she told Duncan.

Duncan looked relieved. "Well, he is awfully big. I guess maybe you get paranoid when you're that big and there's nowhere to hide."

Chrissy collapsed on the floor at the foot of her bed and looked up at Duncan. "I think I'm the one he wants to hide from, too. He thinks I'm out to get him, thanks to you."

"I guess I did make things kind of awkward for you. How about letting me treat you to a pizza to make it up to you?" He reached into the pocket of his brown bomber jacket and pulled out a coupon. "My mom even clipped this out of the paper for us to use."

Chrissy's mind raced for a way to get rid of Duncan without making him suspicious. "I'd like to," she finally said, "but I'm going to Beth's. She said she needs to talk. It sounds like it might be something serious." Chrissy glanced at the clock on her bedside table. It was getting late, and she couldn't afford to waste any more time. "In fact, she's probably wondering where I am right now," she told Duncan.

Duncan stood up. "How about a rain check, then? Maybe tomorrow night?"

Chrissy stood up, too, and began herding Duncan toward the door. "Sorry, I have to work tomorrow."

Duncan stopped in the doorway to the hall. "Friday then?"

"Okay," Chrissy hastily agreed. "Friday."

"Great. I'll pick you up at seven. We won't get a pizza until after the basketball game," Duncan added.

Chrissy scowled. "Wait a minute, I never said anything about going to a basketball game."

"I know you didn't. But I think it's about time you went to a game. You didn't even know who Jeff Henderson was until yesterday. The Hornets are great, and they're really fun to watch. Besides, I have to cover the game for the *Buzzette*."

Chrissy didn't really want to go to a basketball game, but it was obvious that accepting Duncan's invitation was the only way she was going to get him to leave.

"Oh, all right," she said, practically pushing him toward the stairs. "I'll go to the game with you. But you know that basketball really isn't my thing."

Duncan laughed as they headed down the stairs together. "You just think it isn't your thing. For all you really know, basketball could be your destiny," he said, repeating a phrase the coach of the girls' basketball team had used to try to talk Chrissy into trying out when she was a freshman.

"Out!" she said, pretending to be offended as she opened the front door.

Tipping his hat, Duncan said, "Until Friday then."

Chrissy just grinned, pointing toward the Green Pea. Duncan turned and loped off, and Chrissy shut the door after him.

"What did Duncan want?" Mrs. McCall asked, coming into the front hall just as Chrissy started back up the stairs.

"He wanted me to go out for pizza with him," Chrissy said.

Mrs. McCall smiled. "How nice."

Chrissy shrugged. "I guess so. Well, I better get going. Beth's probably wondering where I am."

"Don't forget to be home by eleven."

"I won't," Chrissy assured her. Then she dashed up the stairs. She'd suddenly remembered where her black top was. Now all she had to do was change, pack up her acoustic guitar, and go!

"Sorry I'm late," Chrissy told Robin when he opened the back door to let her into his house.

"There's no such thing as late here," Robin replied as he led the way downstairs to the Jameses' basement.

When they entered the soundproofed practice room, Chrissy was surprised to see that there were at least ten other people besides Robin and his band—and eight of the ten were girls! Chrissy recognized a couple of them from school.

"You know the guys in the band?" Robin asked casually. "Gary, Dave, and Van."

Chrissy nodded. "Hi." Gary, Dave, and Van were gathered around Van's keyboard looking at some sheet music. Glancing up, the boys mumbled a quick hello, then lowered their eyes to the music again.

"And over here," Robin added, waving a hand at the small crowd milling around informally at the other end of the room, "we have the peanut gallery. This is Chrissy McCall, gang." Robin took hold of Chrissy's hand and gave it a squeeze. His touch was electric.

"Chrissy is a songwriter," Robin announced. "If we're nice to her, she might play one or two of her songs for us. How about it, Chrissy?"

Chrissy hadn't expected an audience other than the members of the band. But having an audience had never put her off before. In fact, it always encouraged her. "Sure. I'd love to do a couple of songs," she said.

"Okay then," Robin said, finally letting go of her hand. "Get out your guitar. Maybe we'll try coming in with you, if you don't mind."

"Not at all," she reassured him. "That would be great."

Chrissy took off her pink wool coat and tossed it onto the nearest empty chair. Then she opened up her guitar case and took out her old acoustic guitar. As she slipped her arm through her guitar strap, she suddenly realized that she was auditioning, in a way, and a lump started to form in her throat. This was an important moment, and Chrissy didn't want to blow it.

Standing next to Robin, Chrissy was acutely aware that she was the taller of the two. Then she realized Robin was wearing leather moccasins instead of his usual engineer boots, making him a good two inches shorter. She was just glad she was wearing her black flats instead of something with a heel.

"What key are you going to be playing in?" Gary asked as Chrissy tuned her guitar to Robin's.

"B flat," Chrissy told him. Then she played her intro, walking toward the electric keyboard as she strummed a variation of the tune she'd be singing.

"Play that again, will you?" Robin asked. This time, he played along on his guitar. "That's not the song you were singing at the music store, is it?" he said before Chrissy started singing.

Chrissy shook her head and stopped playing. "I haven't finished that one yet," she explained. "I haven't had time to work on it. But I think you'll like this one."

Robin nodded. "I didn't mean to stop you. I really like the interesting chord progression you've put together on the front. What's this song called, anyway?"

" 'Hello, Stranger,' " Chrissy told him, blushing slightly. Something about Robin's intensity was making her forget that there was anyone else in the room.

Chrissy sang the first verse, and as she launched into the chorus, Gary picked up the beat on the drums. Van joined in on his keyboard when Chrissy began the second verse, and finally Dave joined in on his electric bass. Chrissy found the fuller sound thrilling.

"All right!" Robin said after the last chord had been played. "I like it. It's got the kind of flavor that would be right for us." He turned back to the other guys. "Don't you guys think so?" he asked. Then, not waiting for their reply, Robin turned back to Chrissy. "Of course, before I'd do it, I'd have to change a word here and there to make it more masculine. That wouldn't be a problem for you, would it? I mean, you wouldn't mind if we used your song, would you? It would give you a chance to see how it goes over."

Chrissy smiled. "I'd really like that. Anything you want to do with it is all right with me, too."

"Do that cowbell thing of yours, Gary, you know, at the beginning," Robin commanded excitedly. Then, turning to Dave, he added, "This time, go a little lighter on the bass. I'm going to try joining Chrissy on the chorus. I'm not sure B flat is going to be the right key for me, though."

Gary began hitting the cowbell with a drum stick to her song. Then, as Van and Dave joined in on keyboard and bass, Chrissy sang:

> *Remember how it used to be?*
> *Me and you and you and me.*
> *Where did we go wrong, boy?*
> *Our feelings were so strong.*
> *But now our love is gone, all gone.*

*Now we're just
strangers, strangers.*

*Hello, stranger.
Remember me?
Remember me?
Stranger, hello.*

"Wait up," Robin said, holding his hand over his head. Everyone stopped playing. "Let's start over from the top. I want to hear what it sounds like if I start right out with Chrissy, instead of waiting for the chorus."

Once again, Gary led things off with the cowbell. But this time as Chrissy started to sing, Robin turned so that he was facing her. Looking into his smoldering gray eyes, Chrissy felt she was singing the song for him—and only him.

When they finished, the peanut gallery, as Robin had called their audience, broke into wild applause.

Robin threw back his head and laughed. "Well, Chrissy, I think that means they like it." He slipped his arm around Chrissy's shoulders and gave her a squeeze. His touch made her tingle.

Although Chrissy usually loved the sound of applause, this time she didn't care what anyone else thought. The only person's opinion that mattered to her was Robin's. Something had happened while they were singing to each other, something that had never happened to Chrissy before. She was falling in love!

"Let's try it again, Rob," Van said. "I've got a couple of ideas I'd like to try on the bridge."

As they worked, Chrissy's feelings for Robin grew. She just knew by the way he was looking at her that he felt the same way, too. By the time they'd played "Hello, Stranger" several times, the song had taken on a fast, throbbing beat Chrissy really liked. Playing the guitar side by side with Robin was terrific. It was what she'd always dreamed about doing.

"I need a soda or something." Robin took off his guitar and placed it in its metal stand. Then he pulled a bandanna out of the back pocket of his worn jeans and wiped his damp forehead with it. "How about you, Chrissy? Thirsty?"

Chrissy nodded. "A soda would be great," she said, following him over to the old refrigerator in the corner of the room.

Robin popped open a can of diet cola and handed it to Chrissy. "This okay?" he asked.

"Sure. Thanks," she told him. Then Robin started handing out sodas to the others. Glancing down at her watch, Chrissy saw that it was nearly eleven already! It seemed as if they had barely gotten started. Reluctantly, Chrissy told Robin she had to be going.

"We're practicing again tomorrow, same place, same time," Robin told her as he walked her out to the car. "Can you make it? Maybe we can work on another one of your songs." Robin leaned against the car and touched the tip of Chrissy's nose with his finger. "You do have more songs, don't you?"

Chrissy nodded. "I've got a hundred songs," she assured him, wondering if he might kiss her, and afraid that he would—or that he wouldn't. Then she remembered that she had to work at The Golden Note Thursday night. "But I'm afraid I can't make it tomorrow. I have to work at the store."

"How about stopping by after work?" Robin suggested, straightening up and rubbing his arms in the cold night air.

Chrissy shook her head. She wanted to say yes, but she knew her parents would never let her. "I work too late, and I have homework."

"How about Friday then?" he pressed.

"Sure. Friday night would be good," she said.

Robin opened the car door for her. "Great. See you then!"

Chapter Five

"How did it go?" Beth asked, sliding across the seat of the bus to make room for Chrissy. "You did go to Robin's house last night for the band's rehearsal, didn't you?"

"I did, and it was wonderful." Chrissy sighed. "I'll tell you something if you'll swear you won't repeat it to anyone."

Beth covered her heart with her right hand. "I swear."

"And I mean not *anyone*. Not Avis, not Vicky, not even Paul," Chrissy added.

"Not even Paul," Beth agreed, her hand still over her heart. "I swear. Now tell me!"

"I think I'm in love," Chrissy whispered, leaning back against the green leather bench seat.

"In love?" Beth sounded impressed. "With whom?"

"With Robin James, of course," Chrissy told her indignantly. "Who else?"

Beth laughed. "Just about anyone else. Aren't you the one who's told me at least a thousand times you could never be interested in any boy who wasn't at least six feet tall? Robin can't be more than five foot seven."

"Five foot eight," Chrissy corrected her. "Anyway, lots of tall women go out with shorter men. Look at Christie Brinkley and Billy Joel. Dudley Moore and . . . well, height isn't everything. Being on the same wavelength with a guy is much more important. Besides, Robin usually wears those boots that make him taller. And then, when he sings . . ." Her voice trailed off as she searched for the right words to describe the magic she had felt when she sang with Robin.

Beth nodded earnestly. "I can see what you mean, I guess. So what happened? Did you bring your guitar? Did he ask you to play? What did you wear? Tell me everything!"

Chrissy hugged her books a little tighter as the bus rounded a curve. "I wish you could have been there with me. Then you'd understand. Hey, I have a great idea! Why don't you come to Robin's with me Friday night? There were a bunch of people there last night just listening to us play. Robin had extra chairs set up for them and everything. I'm sure he wouldn't mind if I brought you."

"Then you did play with the band!"

Chrissy nodded. "I played 'Hello, Stranger,' and Robin really liked it. I'm pretty sure the band is going to play it at the Heartthrob Hop."

"Chrissy!" Beth squealed. "That's great! I *love* that song."

"Robin kind of turned it into a duet. Then with the rest of the guys playing, the song had this incredibly full sound. It was like a dream come true, it really was. The kids that were there listening liked it, too. Well, will you come with me?"

"I'd like to. I really would," Beth said. "But I just remembered, I already accepted a date with Paul for Friday night."

"He could come, too," Chrissy suggested. "I'm sure it'll be okay. Of course, he'll have to promise not to say anything about it to Duncan, or anyone else."

Beth laughed. "I don't think Paul even knows Duncan all that well. Anyway, I'll ask him. The thing is, there's a basketball game Friday night. Since Paul knows a lot of the guys on the team, he'll probably want to go to the game."

Chrissy felt all the blood drain out of her face at the mention of the basketball game on Friday night.

"Hey," Beth said, "is something wrong? Do you feel all right?"

Chrissy groaned. "I promised Duncan I'd go to the game with him on Friday night. How am I ever going to get out of that without telling him where I'm going?"

Beth looked sympathetic. "Would it really be so bad if Duncan knew you were working with Robin and the Hoods? He'd probably be just as happy for you as I am."

"Right," Chrissy said wryly. "He'd be so happy that he'd be all over the place taking pictures of me. That would ruin everything."

"I don't know," Beth mused. "Robin might like it. Duncan's pictures would be good publicity for him and the band."

"Well, I don't want to take that chance," Chrissy said stubbornly. "Having Duncan around would be a real drag."

"What I don't understand is why you accepted a date with Duncan when you feel that way about him," Beth said.

"It's not really a date. Duncan dropped by my house last night just when I was getting ready to go to Robin's." Chrissy shook her head at the memory of him suddenly appearing in her room. "Of course my parents just sent him up to my room without telling me he was on his way. Sometimes they are so thoughtless!"

"Your parents really have a thing about getting the two of you together, don't they?" Beth asked.

"Do they ever! It's awful."

"Oh, I don't know," Beth said thoughtfully. "I think Duncan's really funny and nice—"

"Well, anyway," Chrissy interrupted, "if I hadn't said I'd go to the game with him, Duncan *never* would have left. Beth, what am I going to do? I don't want to go to the basketball game. I even tried to tell Duncan that, but he never takes no for an answer. But how am I going to get out of it without making him suspicious?"

"This is a tough one," Beth agreed. "If you really don't want Duncan to find out about Robin, you'd better just go to the game with him. Besides, you did make those plans first. Robin will probably understand. You can go to another rehearsal."

Chrissy sighed. "But that's not what I want to do," she said as the bus pulled up in front of the high school. "If only there were some way I could . . ." As Chrissy stood up to get off the bus, she had a sudden inspiration. "I've got it!" she cried, turning around on the steps and blocking Beth's way.

"Uh-oh," Beth said, her blue eyes growing round. "I know that look, Chrissy McCall. It means that I'm about to get in trouble. Maybe I should just say no before you even have a chance to ask me to help you with one of your crazy schemes."

"Please, Beth," Chrissy pleaded. "I really need your help. You know I wouldn't ask if this weren't important to me."

"Oh, all right," Beth relented. "I guess hearing you out won't hurt anything. What do you want me to do?"

"I don't know what *she* wants you to do," the bus driver said, interrupting their conversation, "but *I* want you both to get off the bus now. I've got more people to pick up and deliver this morning, you know."

Chrissy looked around and saw that the bus was empty except for the three of them. "Sorry," she said sheepishly, and hopped off the bus, with Beth right behind her.

The two girls giggled as they dashed into the school. "Talk about embarrassing!" Beth said, rolling her eyes. "Well, guess I'll see you at lunch."

Chrissy grabbed Beth's sleeve. "Wait a minute. You said you'd hear me out. I'm not letting you escape this easily."

"Okay," Beth said with a sigh. "What do you want me to do?"

But a million kids were swarming around them, and Chrissy decided that the front foyer of Edmond High wasn't the best place to discuss her plans, not if she wanted to keep them secret.

"I guess maybe we should talk about the details later." Chrissy nodded nervously at the crowd. "I will tell you this much, though. I have a plan that will let me be both places on Friday, but I need your help to carry it off."

"I can't wait to find out how you plan to be two places at once," Beth said, smiling.

"Well, just get to the cafeteria a little early, before everyone else shows up. I'll tell you then."

"Okay. See you at lunch!" Then Beth turned and disappeared up the stairs to the second floor.

It was going to be tricky, Chrissy thought to herself as she headed for her homeroom, but with Beth's help, she was sure she'd be able to pull it off. She had to!

"Okay, I'll do it," Beth said, poking at her taco salad, "but I'm not exactly thrilled about it. I'll admit Duncan can be a little ditzy, but I'm not sure he deserves this kind of treatment, Chrissy. All in all he's really been a pretty good friend to you. Remember what you said yourself about backing out on plans with friends?"

"I also say 'All's fair in love and war,'" Chrissy reminded her friend. "Beth, I could feel something really intense between Robin and me the minute we started singing together. If Duncan jumps in now, Robin could end up feeling the same way about me that Jeff Henderson does!"

"Jeff Henderson, the basketball player?"

Chrissy nodded. "Ever since Duncan took that picture of us under the bleachers, Jeff runs every time he sees me."

Beth giggled. "Really? What a riot!"

Chrissy couldn't help laughing, too. "I guess it is kind of funny. But it wouldn't be if I *liked* Jeff."

"I guess I see what you mean. Uh-oh." Beth nodded toward the cafeteria doors. "Here come Avis and Vicky. We'd better change the subject if you don't want them to know what you're up to."

"I'm going to tell them eventually," Chrissy assured Beth. "Just not yet."

"You'll never guess what's happened!" Vicky exclaimed as she set her tray down next to Chrissy's a few minutes later.

"Dave Mullen finally asked you to the Heartthrob Hop," Chrissy guessed.

Vicky grinned. "Last night."

"That's great, Vicky," Beth told her.

"Thanks. Now we can all go together, just like we planned." Then Vicky looked at Chrissy. "But what about you?"

"She can come with us, too," Beth said. "Right, Chrissy?"

"Maybe," Chrissy said, thinking of Robin and the Hoods. If they were going to be playing her music, she might end up going to the dance with them. Maybe she could help with their equipment or maybe she could even sing with them! After all, Robin had turned her song into a duet. She was definitely going to do her best to bring up the subject when she saw him again Friday night.

"Hey, Chrissy. I'm talking to you," Avis said, tapping Chrissy on the arm. With a toss of her head, she sent her long, reddish-blond hair over her shoulder. "Are you having an out-of-body experience, or what?"

"I'm sorry. I was thinking about the dance," Chrissy replied. "It's still more than a week away. Maybe I'll have my own date by then, and I won't need to tag along with you guys."

"That would be perfect, wouldn't it?" Vicky asked excitedly. "All of us together with our dates!" She flashed everyone a big smile as she speared a forkful of her taco salad.

"Everybody smile like Vicky," Duncan commanded, stopping near their table to take a group picture. Then, without waiting to be invited, he pulled out a chair and sat down. "What's up, girls?"

"We were just talking about the Heartthrob Hop," Vicky told him. "Are you going, Duncan?"

Looking at Chrissy, Duncan said, "I've been thinking about it. I hear the band they've booked for it is really good." Chrissy felt herself blush as she quickly looked away. For a second she was afraid Duncan knew that she had rehearsed with Robin, but she knew that was impossible. Wasn't it?

"Robin and the Hoods," Avis told him. "They played at River Fest last summer. You must have heard them. They're great!"

"I heard that they've been doing a lot of birthday parties and stuff like that, too," Vicky commented. "I think Sue Sherman had them play at that Christmas party she had for the seniors at the country club. Apparently, that's when Wally Annon decided to hire them for the Heartthrob Hop. He's the chairman of the entertainment committee, you know."

"You seem to know a lot about them, Vicky," Duncan commented, his green eyes taking on that mischievous glint that tended to make Chrissy nervous.

Vicky shrugged. "Dave's older sister Emma knows Gary Tripp, their drummer. He graduated from Edmond last year, you know."

"Vicky's going to the dance with Dave," Chrissy explained to Duncan.

"All the guys in the band graduated from here last year, including Robin James," Avis added. Then she laughed. "The funny thing is, they were sort of social outcasts while they were going to school here. But now that they've graduated, all the cheerleader types are hiring them to play at their birthday parties."

Chrissy had to bite her tongue to keep from jumping into the conversation. Obviously, her friends didn't understand the kind of life musicians led. She wanted to straighten them out, but she knew she'd just have to wait.

"Well, I better move along. Who knows what great pictures are waiting out there for me? I'd hate to miss one," Duncan said, getting to his feet.

Once he was gone, Vicky shook her head and said, "Duncan is so sweet. I can't believe he isn't dating someone."

"I can," Avis said. "He's always wearing that silly hat of his and taking pictures without warning."

"He warned us today," Chrissy said, surprised to hear herself defending him.

"I guess," Avis admitted. "But he didn't give us a choice. I mean, he just said 'Smile' and then—click!"

"Say, he wasn't wearing his hat," Vicky observed. "I wonder why?"

"Mr. Beckworth told him he couldn't wear it during school anymore," Beth told her. "He said the hat was distracting. I guess a few teachers must have complained."

"Well, I think his hat's cute," Vicky said. "If I weren't going to the dance with Dave, I might see if I couldn't get Duncan to ask me."

"Really?" Chrissy asked, surprised.

Vicky nodded. "But it probably wouldn't work anyway. I think he's interested in you, Chrissy."

"Don't be silly," Chrissy said quickly. "We're just friends. Or at least, our parents are friends. We've sort of been forced on each other, if you know what I mean."

"I do," Beth assured her.

"Me, too," Avis agreed. "I hate that. My parents think that just because they like someone, I should automatically like their friend's kid, male or female, no matter how dorky that kid is."

"Duncan isn't dorky," Chrissy said defensively. Then she added, "But I know what you mean, Avis. Parents can be pretty dense at times."

"I wonder who Duncan is thinking of inviting to the Hop," Vicky mused.

"Well, whoever it is, he'd better hurry up and ask her," Avis said. "Time is definitely running out."

Chapter Six

At The Golden Note, business was usually slow on Thursdays around dinnertime, and this Thursday was no exception. At Mr. Levi's prompting, Chrissy had taken out a box of pitch pipes and was hanging them up on a little tabletop rack. As she worked, she hummed the tune of "Hello, Stranger," imagining as she did that Robin was singing with her.

The more she thought about it, the more she realized how great the two of them were together. She hoped Robin was having similar thoughts. It wasn't hard for Chrissy to imagine him taking her hands in his . . . "Join the band, Chrissy," he would say. "We'll tour the world together."

First they would travel all across the USA, then Europe. Then Japan and South America and Australia. They'd pick up new musical ideas along the way. Chrissy would keep writing songs. But mostly, she and Robin would be together. They'd be famous for the intensity of their love duets.

Chrissy sighed and closed her eyes. She visualized Robin and herself up on stage with thousands of fans at their feet, screaming for more. Then she heard Robin gently call her name . . .

"Chrissy?" This time a gentle touch on the arm went along with the voice, and Chrissy's eyes popped open.

"Robin!" she cried, amazed to see him. It was almost as if the power of her imagination had conjured him up. "What are you doing here?"

Robin laughed. "Actually, I came to hang out—and to get a couple sets of metal finger picks for Dave."

"I'll get the picks for you," Chrissy said, setting the box of pitch pipes down.

"Wait," Robin said. This time when he touched her arm, he let his hand remain there. "I wanted to talk to you. Do you get a break soon? Maybe I could buy you a soda or something."

Chrissy glanced quickly at her wristwatch. Mr. Levi was due back from his dinner break any minute. Becky was scheduled to go next, but she might be willing to trade times with Chrissy. If Robin bought her a soda, it would be their first date! Chrissy simply couldn't pass that one up.

"Let me check with Becky," she said eagerly. "I'm pretty sure I can work something out."

Robin nodded, and Chrissy hurried over to the register where Becky was busy unpacking sheet music.

"Sure," Becky agreed easily, peering over Chrissy's shoulder to get a better look at Robin. "I remember hearing his band last summer at River Fest. I was working the breakfast shift at Finnegan's then, and they were set up right outside the restaurant. They're pretty good." Then she grinned at Chrissy. "Are you two an item?" she asked, wiggling an eyebrow.

Chrissy felt her cheeks color. "Not yet," she said truthfully. "But soon, I hope. Don't tell anyone, though. Okay?"

Becky nodded. "Your secret's safe with me. Well, here comes Mr. Levi. I guess you can go."

"Thanks. I owe you one."

"I can go," Chrissy told Robin just as Mr. Levi walked back into the store.

"Great. You probably know this mall better than I do. Where's a good place?" Robin asked.

"How about that Mexican fast food place?" Chrissy suggested. "They're never very busy, and they don't care how long you sit there as long as you buy something first."

Robin nodded. "Sounds perfect."

While Robin went to the counter to get a couple of drinks for them, Chrissy found a table at the back.

"Here you go," Robin said, handing Chrissy the plastic cup. "One large diet cola. I got us some nachos to share, too."

Chrissy smiled. "Thanks."

Robin sat down across from her. "Actually, I'm the one that should be thanking you. Your song was great. I wish you could have heard everyone raving about it after you left last night."

"Thanks," Chrissy said shyly.

Robin shook his head and chuckled. "There you go, thanking me again. Look, I'll be honest with you, Chrissy. Robin and the Hoods means everything to me. I think we can make it. We've had some good reviews around the state and we're ready to do a lot more. The trouble is, none of us is very good at songwriting. We need a lot of new material now, songs with some substance that go well with our original sound."

"I know just what you're talking about," Chrissy said eagerly.

"You do? That's great!" Reaching across the table, Robin covered Chrissy's hands with his own. Chrissy felt as though he'd started a fire that traveled up her arms all the way to her heart. "I was hoping we could work something out. We'd like to do 'Hello, Stranger' at the Heartthrob Hop."

Chrissy nodded earnestly. "I never dreamed that song would work so well as a duet."

"A duet?" Robin repeated.

"You know, with the two of us going back and forth with it like that. I guess because I like Angelina so much, I always thought of myself as a solo act, you know, like she is. But I started thinking about it after I left your place last night, and a lot of my songs would make great duets."

"Duets, huh?" Robin repeated thoughtfully. "Why not?" Then he turned to glance at the clock behind the counter. "I've got to go. We start rehearsal soon. You coming tomorrow night?"

"Definitely," Chrissy answered.

"Good." Robin stood up. "I'll see you then. Bring as many songs as you can dig up, and we'll see what we can do with them, okay?"

Chrissy nodded. "You can count on it."

Robin suddenly bent down and gave Chrissy a quick kiss on the cheek. "I can't believe I met you, Chrissy McCall. I must be doing something right to deserve this kind of lucky break." Then he turned and strode off, the heels of his black cowboy boots making a clicking noise on the red tile floor.

Chrissy leaned back in her chair and took a slow sip of her drink. She wasn't just going to go to the dance with the band, she was going to sing with them! And not just one song, either.

On top of all that, Robin had kissed her—even if it was only on the cheek. Everything was falling into place. Her music career, her love life . . . everything!

Chapter Seven

"What are we waiting for?" Chrissy asked Duncan impatiently. "Let's go."

So far everything had gone smoothly enough. Beth and Paul had swung by early, and Chrissy had put her guitar and music in the trunk of Paul's car. They had left her house a few minutes before Duncan arrived. But now Duncan was just sitting behind the wheel of the Green Pea, letting the engine idle, going nowhere.

"We've got a few minutes," Duncan told her. He was staring straight at the river behind Chrissy's house.

"If we get there early, you can take pictures of the crowd. I know you love those crowd shots," Chrissy insisted.

"You seem awfully eager to get to that basketball game. I thought you didn't even like basketball." Duncan turned toward Chrissy and eyed her suspiciously.

Chrissy shrugged. "Maybe I'm beginning to see the merits of the game."

Duncan's sandy eyebrows shot up. "This doesn't have anything to do with Jeff Henderson, does it?"

"Jeff Henderson?" Chrissy wrinkled her nose. "What do you mean?"

Duncan gazed in the direction of the river again. "Well, he is tall. I just thought maybe you'd decided you were interested in him."

"I'd be out of luck if I were. The guy thinks I'm a walking disaster, thanks to you," Chrissy said, following Duncan's gaze. She could see what looked like a bonfire flickering on the island closest to the McCalls' house.

"I wonder who's out there," he said.

"Could be just about anybody."

"I used to think of that as *our* island," Duncan told her. "Remember that winter we built a huge snow fort out there?"

Chrissy couldn't help smiling. They'd spent all winter making the place perfect—only to have it melt in March. She and Duncan had shared a certain intensity that winter she knew she'd never forget. "I wonder if that fort was really as wonderful as I remember."

Duncan turned toward her again. "Of course it was. It was fantastic!"

They sat in silence for a minute or two, then Duncan said, "Are you going to the Heartthrob Hop?"

"What do you mean?" Chrissy asked.

"I mean, do you have a date?"

"A date?" Chrissy repeated. She wished there were some easy way to change the subject, but she couldn't think of one. She couldn't tell Duncan that she was planning on performing at the dance.

"A date, you know, like with a guy? I know you were planning on going with your girlfriends, but it sounds like they all made other plans. I know you really like the band that's playing. So, I thought that if you didn't have a date lined up yet, you might consider going with me."

"It's really nice of you to offer and everything." Chrissy shifted her weight uncomfortably on the car seat. "But I've decided I'm not going."

"Really? But I thought you couldn't wait to hear Robin and the Hoods play."

"I know, but as it turns out, I have to work that night," Chrissy hastily explained, hoping Duncan would buy her story. Besides, she would be working, in a way.

Duncan pushed back his fedora and stared into Chrissy's eyes, making her feel a little like a butterfly pinned to a board. "That doesn't make sense, Chrissy. The dance is next Saturday night at eight o'clock. The mall where you work closes at *six* Saturday nights."

"We're doing our yearly inventory after the store closes," Chrissy improvised.

Putting the car in gear, Duncan started backing down the driveway. "Well, it's too bad you'll have to miss one of your favorite bands."

"That's just part of having a job, I guess," Chrissy said cheerfully. She was relieved that Duncan was willing to believe her story. Even if he was mad when he found out the truth, it was going to be worth it, she told herself. Besides, she'd find a way to make it up to him somehow.

"There isn't a single place to park!" Chrissy cried as Duncan made a third trip through the school parking lot.

"We should have gotten here earlier." He pulled out of the lot and drove down a side street. "It's my fault. We shouldn't have sat around in your driveway for such a long time."

"That's okay," Chrissy assured him. She had spotted Paul Brady's car parked right near the side entrance, and she started to get excited about the evening ahead—the part with Robin, anyway. "I don't mind walking."

"Good. Because I'll also need you to help me lug my equipment over to the gym. This isn't just a pleasure outing for me," he reminded her. "I'm here to cover the game for the *Buzzette*."

"Sure," Chrissy replied easily. "How much stuff do you have?"

Duncan nodded toward the backseat and Chrissy looked over her shoulder. "Good grief!" she cried. "What *is* all that?"

"A bag of lenses, some film, an extra camera, two flash attachments . . ." Duncan rattled off the list as he slipped the Green Pea into a tight spot between two vans.

Chrissy laughed. "All right, already. I get the *picture*!"

"You're certainly *long* on puns, aren't you?" Duncan shot back.

Chrissy punched him in the arm. "Is that another one of your tall jokes?"

"Ouch!" Duncan cried, grabbing his arm in mock pain. "Watch the violence, McCall! I would have thought you, of all people, were *above* that sort of thing."

"There you go again!" Chrissy yelled, giving him another light punch.

Duncan threw open the car door and hopped out. "Help! Help!" he called to no one in particular.

"Shh!" Chrissy ordered, springing out after him. "Someone will hear you."

Duncan chuckled. "I'll quit if you will."

Chrissy opened the back door of the car. "Just what do you want me to carry?" she asked.

"You can take the lenses and the extra camera. Be careful—they're really fragile."

By the time they got to the gym, it was as packed as the lot had been.

"What's the big deal?" Chrissy asked, looking around. She had no idea that basketball was so popular in Edmond.

"I told you, the team is really hot this year. They're rated third in the state. They've nearly got our conference title sewn up and are looking to the regionals. From there, it's the state tournament in the cities," Duncan explained.

"Go, Hornets!" the cheerleaders yelled, waving their green and white pom-poms furiously at the crowd. "Go! Fight! Win!"

"I like to stay down here," Duncan said. Pushing his hat to the back of his head, he nodded at the space between the bleachers and the basketball court. "I get the best pictures when I can keep moving around, trying different angles."

Chrissy put Duncan's equipment down next to him, then scanned the bleachers for Beth and Paul. As soon as she located them, she said, "I'll stay with you for a while. Then I might go up and sit with Beth."

Duncan smiled appreciatively. "Great. It'll be more fun for me with you around."

All at once a horn sounded, and seconds later the team began jogging onto the gym floor. Jeff

Henderson was leading the team. As he passed Chrissy she grinned at him, and Jeff's mouth dropped open as if he had seen a ghost.

As usual, Duncan caught the whole scene on film. Lifting his head from the camera, he jabbed Chrissy playfully in the ribs with his elbow. "How does it feel to make such a good impression?" he asked.

Chrissy giggled. "I just hope I don't mess up his game."

Duncan nodded thoughtfully. "Maybe you'd better forget staying down here with me. In fact, maybe you better just go back to the car."

"Are you kidding? It's ten degrees out there! I'll freeze!"

"Oh, well. I guess Jeff will just have to get over this phobia of his," Duncan teased, focusing his camera for the next shot.

"I'm sure it didn't help when he saw you here with me," Chrissy told Duncan. "He probably thinks the two of us are a team. I set the trap, and you shoot the picture."

"Great idea!" Duncan cried, snapping a picture of the tip-off.

Chrissy stuck out her tongue at him. "I could almost believe you're serious."

"I almost am," he admitted just as Jeff took an inside shot and sank the first basket. The crowd went wild. Duncan hurried toward the other end of the court and Chrissy followed him.

The action up and down the court was so fast and furious that Chrissy was finally forced to sit down. But Duncan kept right up with the team. At times, Chrissy could have sworn there were two of him.

When the buzzer signaling halftime sounded, Duncan headed over to the spot where Chrissy was sitting. She was trying to figure out just how to get rid of him so she could sneak out with Beth and Paul when he said, "I ran out of film. I'm going to have to run up to the *Buzzette* office for more. Want to come with me?"

Chrissy shook her head. "I'm going to get something to drink." She forced out a feeble cough. "My throat feels kind of funny."

"Really?" Duncan looked concerned. "Are you okay?"

"I'll be fine," Chrissy said breezily. "Don't worry about me. You've got your job to do, and I don't want to get in the way."

"I'll be right back," he told her. "If you don't feel better after you get something to drink, I'm going to either find someone to take you home or take you home myself."

Chrissy smiled. Fooling Duncan was turning out to be easy, maybe even too easy. She watched him leave the gym, then she quickly scaled the bleachers.

"Hi, Beth. Hi, Paul," Chrissy said. "I'm all ready to go."

Beth sighed. "I was really hoping you'd change your mind about leaving early. Don't you think now that you're certain you're singing with the band at the dance, you should just tell Duncan about it? He'd probably be glad to take you to Robin's himself."

"That's just what I *don't* want!" Chrissy exclaimed, sitting down with them. "Even if Duncan wouldn't create a scene taking pictures of the band, I still don't want to have to explain about him to Robin. It's just easier this way. Believe me."

Paul stood up and fished his car keys out of his pocket. "I'm going to let you take the car, Beth. I don't want to miss any of this game."

"Okay," Beth quickly agreed. But Chrissy could tell she wasn't happy about Paul's decision to stay there by himself.

"Sorry, Beth," Chrissy said as they hurried outside. "I hope I haven't ruined your date with Paul."

"I don't know why I let you get me into these situations in the first place," Beth complained. "I should have known Paul wouldn't want to leave the game early, when it came right down to it."

"Come on, Beth!" Chrissy urged as she waited

for Beth to unlock the car. "Robin only lives about five minutes from here. After you drop me off, you can come right back."

"Leaving Paul is only part of it, Chrissy. I'm not very happy about lying to Duncan, either. I mean, I think it's bad enough that *you* are."

"You won't be lying, not really. I really don't feel very good," Chrissy said. "I feel totally nervous. I guess you don't know how important this is to me."

"That's where you're wrong," Beth said as she started Paul's car. "I do know, and I think it's great. But I also think you've blown Duncan's ability to mess things up for you totally out of proportion."

"You didn't see Jeff Henderson's face tonight when he ran out onto the court and saw me standing there, did you?" Chrissy said.

Beth shook her head. "I guess I missed that."

"Well, he was freaked out to say the least. And all because of Duncan. I don't want Robin to think that I've got this guy with a camera joined at my hip," Chrissy insisted stubbornly.

"Well, here we are." Beth pulled over to the curb in front of Robin's house. "This is the place, isn't it?"

Chrissy nodded. Her stomach felt as if it had been invaded by a swarm of butterflies, and her throat was completely dry. "This is it," she managed to say as she opened the car door and got out. Beth opened the trunk and Chrissy took her guitar and folder of sheet music. "I really appreciate this, Beth."

"I know," Beth assured her. "Now, go in there so I can get back to Paul. And good luck!"

Chrissy smiled. "Thanks. Have fun with Paul! I'll talk to you tomorrow." Then she slammed the trunk shut and hurried toward the house, giving Beth one last wave as she reached the doorstep.

"I was hoping it was you," Robin said, opening the door for Chrissy only seconds after she'd rung the bell.

Chrissy felt all her doubts and misgivings melt away as she looked into Robin's eyes. He was obviously as glad to see her as she was to see him. Chrissy knew she had done the right thing by keeping her date to rehearse with him.

"Did you bring more songs with you?" he asked eagerly as she followed him downstairs.

"I sure did," she told him.

"I hope they're all as good as 'Hello, Stranger,' " he said, smiling.

As they entered the practice room in the basement, Chrissy was surprised to see only Gary, Van, and Dave there. "Where is everyone?" she asked Robin.

He ran a hand through his short, jet-black hair. "I thought we might be able to get more done without anyone to distract us. The dance is a week from tomorrow, you know. That doesn't give us much time. I told the guys you might be singing with us."

"Might?" Chrissy repeated, a little taken aback.

"Yeah, well, I think there are some things that need to be worked out before that can happen." Robin strapped on his guitar. "But I'm sure it'll all work out. So, let's hear another song of yours. Then we'll play our version of 'Hello, Stranger' for you."

Chrissy laid her guitar case on a ratty-looking, overstuffed chair and opened it. "The first song I thought I'd do is called 'Dream Boy.' We could change the lyrics if you think it would make a good duet."

"Don't worry too much about your songs making good duets," Robin told her.

Chrissy saw Van and Gary exchange looks. Something funny was going on, but she couldn't figure out exactly what.

"We'll do pretty much what we did Wednesday," Robin told her. He sounded a little nervous. "You start the song, Chrissy, and we'll join in at some point, okay?"

Chrissy nodded. Then she played the first few chords. Taking a deep breath, she started to sing:

All I do is dream of you.
Day and night, I dream of you.

Oh, dream
dream, dream, dream.
Oh, dream
dream, dream, dream.

"Wait," Robin said just as Van started playing a flashy bridge on his electric keyboard. Van stopped playing and so did Chrissy. "I don't like that one too much. The tune is good, but the lyrics are sort of sophomoric, don't you think?"

Chrissy felt her cheeks color. "I've got others," she said, trying to act professional even though Robin's words had stung her.

"Good." Robin pulled over a stool and sat down. "Let's hear something else then. We can always go back to that one if we have to. What I'd really like is to have three of your best for next Saturday."

Chrissy nodded. "This one is called 'Meant to Be.' " Her feelings had been hurt by Robin's reaction to "Dream Boy," but she tried to tell herself that she was being silly. If she wanted to be a pro like Robin, she couldn't be so sensitive about every little lyric.

"I like that title," Robin told her, nodding.

Chrissy smiled at his compliment. Then, taking a deep breath, she sang:

Hey, boy!
What do you say, boy?

Are we meant to be?
Am I for you? Are you for me?
I want you to know that I think so.
Hey, boy!

The other night
when you held me tight
it was so right
so very right.
You must know it's true.
I just know you do.
You're for me and I'm for you.

As Chrissy started singing the chorus again, Robin joined in, just as he had on Wednesday when they'd sung "Hello, Stranger" together. As their voices blended, the wonderful feeling Chrissy had experienced then returned.

"All right!" Robin exclaimed when they finished. He grabbed Chrissy and gave her a hug. "That's more like it!"

Van smiled. "Nice, Chrissy."

"It'll take a little work," Robin said thoughtfully. "But I think we can make that one excellent. Now we just need one more, Chrissy. What have you got?"

Chrissy thought for a moment. She was almost afraid to present another song because she dreaded getting the kind of reaction she'd gotten on "Dream Boy." "Well," she finally said,

"I do have that one I'm still working on, the one you heard in the store. It's called 'For Beth' because my friend Beth kind of inspired it. But I'm willing to change the title if you don't like it."

"Maybe we should work on 'Meant to Be' before Chrissy gives us a new tune, Rob," Dave suggested.

Chrissy nodded, grateful for Dave's intervention. "I'd rather wait until the other one's ready, if you don't mind."

"I guess that's okay," Robin said, but he sounded disappointed. "I suppose we should really work on staging a bit, too. If we're going to sing these songs together, Chrissy, we're going to have to iron out a few visual problems."

Gary played a little drum roll. "What Robin means is that he's got to figure out how to deal with being short!" He and the other guys laughed, but Robin looked irritated.

"I could sit down," Chrissy offered, blushing. "Or I could wear flats and you could wear your boots." She wanted to show Robin that she wasn't happy about being taller than him, either!

"I guess we'll figure something out," Robin said with a shrug. "Okay then, let's take it from the top."

Chrissy started singing again, but she felt that something important was missing. Both she and Robin were singing, but they weren't singing together. Something was obviously bothering Robin. Chrissy thought she must have done or said something terribly wrong, but she had no idea what.

The song ended, and Robin walked wordlessly to the back of the room. He stood there for a moment, staring at the posters on the wall. Then he turned and walked right past Chrissy and the guys, finally disappearing up the stairs. Stunned, Chrissy looked at Dave, but he just gave her a sympathetic smile and shrugged.

Chapter Eight

When the front doorbell rang Saturday morning, Chrissy's mother jumped up from the breakfast table to answer it. "I wonder who that could be?" she commented as she crossed the kitchen.

"Probably the Girl Scouts," Mr. McCall said with a chuckle. "It's about that time of year again, isn't it? If it is them, get three boxes of the mint cookies. Or is that enough? What do you think, Chrissy?"

"Three sounds about right," Chrissy agreed, too tired to even look up from her cereal bowl. She hadn't gotten home from Robin's until late. It had been a very confusing night. He had been so gruff while they were rehearsing, but when she had left his house to catch a ride home with Van, he had said goodbye cheerfully enough. Something was bothering him, that much was obvious.

"Come on in, Duncan," Mrs. McCall said. "Chrissy's in the kitchen." Chrissy set her spoonful of cereal back in her bowl and shuddered slightly. She had suddenly lost her appetite. She knew she had to get rid of Duncan before her parents discovered that she had been lying, which they were bound to do if Duncan uttered much more than a friendly greeting.

"Hi, Chrissy," Duncan said as he walked into the kitchen. "How are you feeling this morning? Better, I hope."

"Much better," she agreed, getting to her feet and carrying her breakfast dishes to the sink.

Mr. McCall's forehead wrinkled with concern. "Haven't you been feeling well, honey?" he asked.

"I had a little headache last night. Probably from all that cheering at the basketball game. Nothing major, really." Chrissy took hold of the sleeve of Duncan's leather jacket and started pulling him toward the door. "As long as you're here, Duncan," she said, "you can drive me to the mall."

"I really came to talk to *all* of you," Duncan said, resisting Chrissy's efforts to remove him. "My parents want you all to have dinner with us tomorrow."

"How nice," Mrs. McCall said with a smile. "Should I give your mother a call?"

"Sure," Duncan said. "That would be great. I just wanted to come over early to make sure Chrissy knew about it before she left for work. I was hoping I could talk you into going skating before dinner tomorrow. How about it, Chrissy?"

Chrissy was reluctant to agree too quickly. With everything up in the air the way it was, she didn't want to commit herself to anything that might conflict with band rehearsals. But everyone was staring at her, waiting for an answer. None of them knew about her involvement with Robin, and she wanted to keep it that way.

"Okay," she said cheerfully. "That sounds like fun. Well, come on. Let's go, Duncan. I don't want to be late for work."

"I thought you didn't have to be at work until noon. It's only ten o'clock," her mother pointed out.

"I told Mr. Levi I'd come in a little early," Chrissy said, aware that she was lying again. Her mother had once warned her that if she lied, things would snowball so that she'd end up telling one lie after another. Her mother was right! Chrissy hated lying, but she told herself she was doing it for a good reason—her career as a musician could depend on it!

"I said I'd take you," her father said.

"But now that Duncan's here," Chrissy said, "he might as well take me."

Duncan shrugged. "I don't mind, Mr. McCall. There are a couple of things I need to pick up at the mall anyway."

"Should we plan to swing by for you at six then?" Mrs. McCall asked as she poured herself a cup of coffee.

"That would be great," Chrissy said, edging toward the front hall and dragging Duncan with her. "Bye!"

When they were finally sitting in the Green Pea, Duncan turned toward Chrissy and said, "What was all that about?"

"What do you mean?" she asked defensively.

"You were sure in a hurry to get out of there," Duncan commented. "I mean, you practically pulled me out the door. And I thought you had a sore throat last night, not a headache."

"Actually, I had both. But I didn't really want my parents to know about it," Chrissy explained. "I didn't want them worrying. Besides, I was afraid they'd make me stay home from work today if they knew."

"I guess that makes sense. I'm sorry for giving you the third degree," Duncan apologized. He started the car and began backing down the McCalls' long driveway.

"That's okay. No harm done."

"You are okay, aren't you?" Duncan asked once they were cruising down the road. "You still look a little pale. Maybe you've got the flu or something. Maybe you *should* think about staying home from work today."

"I'm fine," Chrissy assured him. "I'm just a little bit tired, that's all. I guess I stayed up too late last night playing my guitar." At least that much wasn't a lie. "It kind of made my head feel better."

"It's been a long time since I've heard you sing one of your songs," Duncan mused. "Maybe you can bring your guitar with you tomorrow."

"Maybe," Chrissy said noncommittally. She didn't even want to go to Duncan's house for dinner.

Once they reached the mall, Duncan pulled up to the entrance nearest The Golden Note and put the Green Pea in neutral.

"Aren't you coming in?" Chrissy asked, trying not to sound as relieved as she felt. She really didn't need to be at work until noon, but she would have had to go into the store if Duncan had parked to walk with her.

Duncan shook his head. "I might later. I have to get some stuff for school at the camera store across the street first."

"Thanks a lot for the ride, Duncan," she said as she unbuckled her seat belt and stepped out of the car.

"See you tomorrow," he called after her, "if not sooner!"

* * *

At two o'clock that afternoon, Chrissy had just gone into the back room of the store to take her break when Mr. Levi poked his head in. "There's someone out here who wants to see you," he announced.

"Male or female?" Chrissy joked.

"Male. It's that guy who took you to dinner on Thursday."

"Robin James is out there?" Chrissy cried, leaping to her feet. "Tell him I'll be right out!"

Mr. Levi looked amused. "I'll tell him. I expect you back in the store by two-fifteen, though. I'm sure we're going to be busy this afternoon, and I don't want to be short staffed."

Chrissy nodded. "Don't worry, Mr. L. I'll be back on time."

When Chrissy was alone again, she quickly pulled a brush out of her shoulder bag and ran it through her hair. Just thinking about Robin made her feel nervous, especially now that she knew how cold he was capable of acting when things weren't going the way he wanted them to. Maybe he'd even come to the store to tell her that he'd changed his mind, that she wouldn't be playing at the Heartthrob Hop, because the band didn't want to use her songs after all.

Chrissy took a deep breath to calm herself. Then she tossed her brush back into her purse. Whatever it was, she was ready.

As soon as she stepped into the store, she spotted him. As usual, Robin was dressed all in black except for the neckline of a white T-shirt visible at the collar of his leather jacket. He was leaning against the counter, and he was holding a single red rose.

"Hi," he said when he noticed her walking toward him. He held out the rose. "This is for you. A sort of peace offering."

Chrissy took the flower from him and held it to her nose for a moment. "It's beautiful, Robin. Thanks."

"Yeah, well, the guys told me I was too hard on you last night. In fact, they were pretty upset with me after you left with Van." He paused and looked around nervously. "Want to go somewhere? You're on your break now, aren't you?"

Chrissy nodded. "We could go back to that Mexican place," she suggested.

"That would be okay. We could go somewhere else if there's a place you like better," Robin offered, taking Chrissy's hand.

"I only have about fifteen minutes," Chrissy told him, frowning. His hand felt warm and reassuring. The bad memories of the night before began to fade, and Chrissy knew she still wanted to go out with him.

"Then the Mexican place it is," he said. He gave her hand a gentle squeeze. "I certainly don't want to get my favorite songwriter fired." Chrissy felt herself blush at his compliment.

When they got to the restaurant, Robin bought a couple of soft drinks, and they headed for the table they had sat at the other day. Chrissy laid her rose down gently on the table. The whole thing seemed so romantic: Robin's apology, the rose, sitting at the same table again . . .

"I want to explain why I acted the way I did last night," Robin told her after he'd taken a long drink of his soda.

"It's okay," she assured him. "Don't worry about it."

"No, I want to explain. I think it's important for you to understand where I'm coming from if we're going to work together."

"Okay," Chrissy said. She could hardly argue with that.

"You see, after you left on Wednesday, all those kids that had come to listen to our rehearsal kept raving about your music, but only part of me agreed with them."

"What do you mean?" Chrissy asked, hurt but trying not to show it.

Robin shrugged. "I guess I felt sort of threatened. They'd come to hear *me*, but they were excited about *you*. Then when someone said we ought to change the name of the band to Beauty and the Beasts, I kind of saw red, I guess."

Chrissy laughed. "Beauty and the Beasts? • That's pretty funny!"

Robin smiled faintly. "It is sort of funny, isn't it?" he said sheepishly. "I guess they were probably kidding. But the next day, when you said you wanted to sing with the band . . ." His voice trailed off, and he shrugged.

"You felt like I was trying to take over," Chrissy finished for him. "But I'm not!" *Besides*, she thought, *it only seems fair. After all, you are using my song . . .*

"I know you're not trying to take over. And I think we sound pretty good together, too. The only problem now is, I'm just not sure how we'll look on stage together. I was serious about that last night. I wasn't just trying to give you a hard time."

"I know," Chrissy told him. "I had thought of the same thing, even before you brought it up last night."

"Well, I've done some more thinking about it and I'm pretty sure we can work around it." He took both of Chrissy's hands in his. "Anyway, it's worth a try. The guys in the band really like you."

"How about you, Robin?" Chrissy asked, feeling bold as she gazed into his gray eyes. "How do you feel about me?"

"You know how I feel, don't you?" His voice was soft, almost a whisper.

Chrissy nodded. Looking into Robin's eyes made anything seem possible. Maybe her dream of touring the world with Robin, and singing to sellout audiences, wasn't so farfetched after all.

"Then you'll come back? To our next rehearsal, I mean?" he asked eagerly.

Without hesitation Chrissy said, "Sure. When is it? Tonight?"

Robin shook his head. "We're doing a sweet-sixteen party in Winfield tonight. We'll be rehearsing again tomorrow night, though. Can you make it? We're going to try to get together earlier so we can work longer. Like, about eight o'clock?"

The plans she had made to have dinner at the Wests' flashed through Chrissy's mind, but she hoped that that would be over fairly early. "I'll be there as soon as I can," she promised. Then she glanced at her watch. "I've got to get back to work now," she said reluctantly, getting to her feet.

"Hey, don't forget this," Robin said. He picked up the rose and handed it to her. "Until tomorrow."

"Until tomorrow," Chrissy repeated. Then she turned and hurried away.

Chrissy was just about to go into The Golden Note when she thought she caught a glimpse of Duncan's trademark fedora out of the corner of her eye. When she turned to make sure, though, the hat was gone.

Chapter Nine

"Hurry up!" Duncan's little sister, Annie, urged as Duncan dug her skates out of the back of the Volvo. "We've only got an hour."

"An hour is a lot of time," Chrissy assured the ten-year-old.

"I think Annie would just as soon live on this rink until it closes. Isn't that right, Annie?" Duncan teased, handing Annie her skates.

Annie slung the skates over her shoulder. "Last one on the ice is a rotten egg!" she challenged. Then she took off at a gallop.

"Come on!" Duncan cried. He grabbed Chrissy by the hand, clutching their skates with his other hand. "We can't let Annie win. We'll never hear the end of it. At least I won't. I have to live with her!"

Chrissy's breath came out in little moist puffs as Duncan pulled her along the narrow path. It seemed like forever since she had had time to enjoy the winter. She loved skating, but lately all the fuss over the Heartthrob Hop had turned her schedule from busy to frantic.

By the time Duncan was ushering Chrissy into the warming house, Annie already had her boots off and was pulling on an extra pair of wool socks.

"Slow down, Annie," Duncan ordered.

"No way!" she retorted. "I'm going to beat you today for sure."

"Let her win," Chrissy whispered.

"Are you kidding?" Duncan gasped. He quickly pulled off his own boots. "I wouldn't do that to her. I respect her too much. If she's going to beat me, it'll have to be the real thing."

Chrissy laughed. Only Duncan West would think of going all out to beat a ten-year-old as a matter of honor!

"You better get moving," Duncan warned Chrissy, "or *you* could be the rotten egg."

Chrissy sat down on the bench and hurriedly got into her own skates.

"I win!" Annie cried, dashing out the warming-house door, her red scarf flying out behind her. As the door slammed shut, both Duncan and Chrissy dissolved into uncontrollable laughter.

Finally, Duncan stood up. He looked tall to Chrissy as he bent slightly to offer her a hand up. "We'll go out together. That way we can be rotten eggs together."

"Very noble of you," Chrissy declared with a grin.

When they were finally out on the ice, gliding over the glassy surface, Chrissy felt a sudden burst of happiness. "I love it out here!" she cried, spinning around in a circle. Then she stopped suddenly and snatched Duncan's fedora from his head.

"Hey!" Duncan yelled. "Give that back to me!"

"You'll have to catch me if you want it," Chrissy taunted. She did a quick turn and skated across the enormous rink as fast as she could. She could hear Duncan's blades scratching the surface of the ice as he came after her.

She was practically flying around the rink. Duncan could match her pace, but he couldn't overtake her. Finally, Chrissy came to a breathless stop. "Here," she panted, handing Duncan his hat. "I might be faster, but you're relentless."

Duncan accepted his hat with a sweeping bow, brushing the ice with its brim. "That's because I'm a Taurus, remember?"

"And I'm a Libra with Sagittarius rising." Chrissy skated a circle around Duncan.

"What does that mean?" Duncan asked, following her progress with his eyes.

Chrissy came to a sudden stop. "It means I have long legs."

"Huh?" Duncan looked perplexed.

"Sagittarius rising means I have long legs." Chrissy patted her thighs with her mittened hands. "I guess these legs give me an unfair advantage in some ways. Of course, in other ways," she added, thinking of her talk with Robin about the difference in their heights, "they're something of a curse."

"Never!" Duncan declared fiercely. "You wouldn't be you if you weren't tall. And I wouldn't—"

"Can I play?" Annie asked, sending up a spray of ice as she skidded to a stop between them.

Duncan held Chrissy's gaze before his face broke into an impish grin. "Why, sure." Then his hand flew out and swatted Annie's arm. "You're it!" he cried. With that he turned and skated furiously away. Chrissy followed Duncan's lead, and soon all three of them were flying around the rink, shrieking at each other. Chrissy felt as if she were ten years old again herself, and she loved the feeling.

"You kids look healthy," Mrs. West said, passing Chrissy a plate full of food. "Nice and rosy-cheeked."

Mr. McCall chuckled. "We probably should have gone skating with them."

"I haven't had skates on for years," Mrs. McCall said wistfully. "It probably would have been a disaster."

"I haven't been skating in years either," Mrs. West admitted. "Was the rink crowded, Duncan?"

"By the time we left it was," Duncan said, accepting a plate from her. He looked across the table at Chrissy and winked. "Actually, it was better later. Some of Annie's friends showed up and took her off our hands."

Annie stuck out her tongue at him. "Duncan cheated," she claimed in a singsong voice.

Dr. West laughed. "What did he cheat at this time?"

"Annie made us play tag with her. Then she got mad because she couldn't tag me," Duncan explained. "I guess she would have liked it better if I just *let* her win, even though that would really have been cheating as far as I'm concerned."

"That's what happens when you play with bigger kids," Mrs. West told her daughter. "You wouldn't want Duncan to just let you win, would you, Annie? That would have been what's called a hollow victory."

"No, but I tagged Chrissy and she's even bigger than Duncan," Annie insisted stubbornly.

"Annie!" Duncan shot Chrissy an apologetic look, and she felt herself blush. Obviously he was thinking of the negative comment Chrissy had made about her height that afternoon. He didn't know that when she made it she'd been thinking about how she towered over Robin. Chrissy shifted uncomfortably in her chair. In just a few days she would be able to tell Duncan everything. She was beginning to hate herself for being so deceitful.

"Actually, it was pretty nice of your brother to take you along, Annie." Dr. West eyed his daughter sternly. "I haven't heard you thank him yet either."

"Thank you, Duncan," Annie said grudgingly.

Chrissy caught Duncan's eye and he grinned impishly at her.

"This ham is delicious, Ellie," Mrs. McCall commented in an obvious attempt to change the subject. "Did you get it at Larson's Meat Market?"

The adults started talking about all the different butchers in town, and Chrissy became more and more restless. Because of all the lies she'd been telling lately, she felt as if she were sitting on a powder keg. Suddenly, even though she was having a good time, she wanted to get away as quickly as possible.

"Can I use your phone, Mrs. West?" Chrissy asked, breaking into the conversation. "It's kind of important."

"Certainly. Use the phone in the den, if you like," Mrs. West suggested.

Chrissy got up and hurried toward the Wests' den. Quickly she dialed Beth's number.

"Hello?" Beth answered after a few rings.

"Thank goodness you're home!" Chrissy said.

"Is that you, Chrissy?" Beth asked, her voice filled with concern. "Is something wrong?"

"I'm over at Duncan's with my parents," Chrissy told her. "Do you think you could come over and pick me up? I can't stay here a second longer."

"Well, sure, I guess. I'll have to ask if I can use the car. Hang on. I'll be right back."

While she waited for Beth, Chrissy watched the den door to make sure no one walked in on her conversation.

"I'm back," Beth said a couple of minutes later. "It's okay. How soon should I come?"

"As soon as you can. And remember, if anyone asks, we're going to your house to work on an English project."

"But we're not even in the same class," Beth protested. "Duncan knows that, doesn't he?"

"He might. But we do have the same teacher. Besides, it was the only good reason I could come up with for why I won't be home until late this evening."

"I hope it's okay that I'm a little early," Chrissy said after Beth had dropped her off at Robin's an hour later.

"It's perfect. This way we can work on our staging before the other guys get here." Robin smiled at Chrissy and winked. "I don't want them to accuse me of being too hard on you again."

"I understand," Chrissy said, following him downstairs. "You don't have to go out of your way to be gentle with me. I just want to be one of the guys."

Robin stopped at the bottom of the stairs and turned around to face Chrissy. "You'll never be one of the guys," he told her. "You're much too pretty for that. Now, come on. If we're going to make those love duets of yours work, we've got to make it look as right as it sounds."

A little of the gruffness Robin had shown her Friday night returned as they tried having Chrissy stand various places on the stage. Then Robin got a stool from a corner of the basement, and she tried sitting on that. It made him look taller, but it also looked awkward and staged.

"I think it's time to work on my shoe idea," Chrissy suggested earnestly.

Robin threw back his head and laughed. "You're too much, Chrissy McCall," he declared.

"I m-meant . . ." she stammered.

"I know what you meant," Robin interrupted. He took a step toward her, and Chrissy was almost positive he was about to give her a real kiss at last. But before he could, the doorbell rang. "That must be the guys," Robin said. "I'll be right back."

As soon as Robin left her alone, Chrissy sank back down on the stool. She couldn't help wondering if he really *did* see her as just one of the guys. Were they ever going to be more than singing partners?

Chapter Ten

"It's got to be funky and it's got to be black or at least look good with black," Chrissy said as she parked her father's Chevy at Eastgate Mall on Monday evening. It had started to snow a few minutes earlier, and she watched the big flakes hit the windshield and then melt. "It's got to be flashy but not too flashy. Most of all, it's got to look good with flats."

Beth shook her head. "Sounds like a tall order to me."

"Please!" Chrissy cried, resting her head on the steering wheel. "No tall jokes!"

Beth chuckled as she reached for the door handle. "Sorry. I wasn't trying to make a joke."

"I know." Chrissy got out and walked around the car to join Beth. The girls walked quickly toward the nearest entrance, the snow swirling around them.

"Honestly, Chrissy." Beth opened the glass door and waited for her friend to go in. "I think you're really being a good sport about Robin's height hang-up."

"I really don't think he cares that I'm taller than he is *personally*. It's professionally that he's worried about. I think he's right to worry, too. That's why we're here. When I find the perfect outfit, including the perfect shoes, it's going to make all the difference," Chrissy insisted confidently.

"I hope you're right."

"I know I'm right."

When they reached the central courtyard of the mall, Beth stopped. "I think I know where we should go. It's expensive, though. But you've got plenty of money, or at least, you will soon, right?"

"What do you mean?" Chrissy asked.

"Robin is giving you part of whatever the band's being paid to play at the dance, isn't he?" Beth stopped and faced Chrissy. "Don't tell me he hasn't mentioned that part of it yet?"

"It just hasn't come up," Chrissy said, shrugging. "And anyway, I'm just going to join in on my two songs. I'm not officially a member of the band or anything."

"I guess," Beth conceded. "I just hope he's not going to take advantage of you . . ." She started walking again and didn't stop until they were in front of a store Chrissy had seen before, but never entered. "Here we are. Beverly Eden. This is where Avis says she bought that silk skirt she wore to Vicky's Christmas party."

"I remember that," Chrissy said, nodding. "That skirt was expensive, wasn't it?"

"I told you this place wasn't cheap."

"Well, it can't hurt to look," Chrissy said. "Come on."

As she made her way into the store, Chrissy knew immediately that she had found the right place. Rock music was playing loudly through several speakers, and strategically placed screens featured the latest music videos.

"Do you girls need some help?" a trendy-looking salesclerk asked.

Chrissy was about to answer that they were just looking when a white leather jacket caught her eye. "That," she said, pointing at it. "I have to have that!"

Both Beth and the salesclerk followed her gaze. It only took a few seconds for Chrissy to work her way over to the rack. Anxiously, she lifted the price tag dangling from the sleeve and looked at it.

"Wow!" Beth exclaimed, looking over Chrissy's shoulder at the tag.

"You can say that again! But it's my size." Chrissy took off her pink coat and handed it to

Beth, then slipped on the leather jacket. It even smelled perfect, she decided, grinning.

"Where's the nearest mirror?" she asked.

"Follow me," the clerk said, leading the way.

"Are you really thinking of buying that?" Beth whispered as Chrissy admired her reflection.

Chrissy nodded. "I can wear all black under it—you know, my black jeans and black tank top. And I already have black flats that'll be perfect." She turned sideways to admire her profile. "The guys all wear black leather except for their white T-shirts. I'll be the opposite. I'll be different, but I'll complement them—perfectly. Robin's really going to like this. I just know it."

"But it's so expensive!" Beth pointed out. "Can you afford to buy the other things you need if you get it?"

"If I get this, I won't need anything else," Chrissy told her. Then, turning to the clerk, she said, "I'll take it."

"Cash or charge?" the salesclerk said.

"Cash," Chrissy said, the beginnings of a new song about love on credit taking shape in her mind as she spoke. She smiled. She could hardly wait until the band's next rehearsal. She would wear her new outfit and maybe even play her new song. She'd absolutely win Robin's heart once and for all.

"Where to now?" Beth asked once they'd left the boutique. "What else do you need to get?"

"How about getting something to drink? My treat," Chrissy offered, swinging the black and gold Beverly Eden bag as she walked.

"I meant clothes. I thought we were shopping for an outfit for you."

"I told you already. This is all I need." Chrissy hugged the bag affectionately.

"How about jewelry?" Beth asked. "Don't you need to get something new to wear with the jacket?"

Chrissy shook her head. "I'm going to wear my silver chain necklace and my big silver hoop earrings."

Beth threw up her hands. "All right, then! Let's get a soda."

The girls walked to the sidewalk café in the center of the courtyard and joined the small line of shoppers waiting to be seated. A few minutes later, they were being led to a table for two.

"I feel like celebrating," Chrissy said, closing her menu after a quick glance at it. "How about splitting an order of fries with me?"

"If you're really up for celebrating, let's forget splitting an order and each get our own," Beth suggested with a grin.

"All right!" Chrissy cheered.

"You girls sound awfully happy."

Looking up, Chrissy saw Duncan standing on the other side of the waist-high wall surrounding the café. "What are you doing here?" she demanded.

Duncan looked hurt. "Oh, I'm just fine," he said. "Thank you so much for asking. And how are you?"

"Hi, Duncan," Beth said, giggling.

"Well, hi, Beth. It's nice to see *you*."

"All right," Chrissy said, rolling her eyes. "I get the message." She smiled at Duncan and said, "Hi," while trying to hide her Beverly Eden bag under the table. But she was too late.

"Beverly Eden, huh? Pretty fancy. What'd you buy?" Duncan asked Chrissy.

Chrissy sighed. "Just a jacket."

"If it came from Beverly Eden, it can't be *just* a jacket," Duncan said.

"How do you know so much about Beverly Eden?" Chrissy asked.

Duncan looked at Beth and winked. "I'm a photojournalist, remember? It's my job to know." Duncan started stepping over the barrier that separated them. "Say, would you girls mind if I joined you?"

"As a matter of fact—" Chrissy began. But Beth cut her off.

"Of course not. Pull up a chair," Beth offered cheerfully. As Duncan turned his back for a second to get a chair from a neighboring table, Chrissy shot Beth a dirty look.

"I've got some big news," Duncan told them

114

after he sat down. "Want to take a couple guesses at what it is?"

"No," Chrissy said.

"I bet it has something to do with photography, right?" Beth offered.

Duncan nodded. "I just found out that I'm going to be the official photographer for the Heartthrob Hop."

"What does that mean?" Chrissy asked, staring at Duncan with disbelief.

"It means that I'm going to record the highlights of the dance for the memories section of the *Echowan*."

"That's great, Duncan. Have you got a date for the dance then?" Beth asked.

"Not yet," Duncan admitted. Suddenly, he looked right at Chrissy. "But I haven't given up. Of course, I'll be working. The girl I take will have to understand that."

Just then the waitress returned with their drinks and fries. "Can I get you something?" she asked Duncan.

"No, thanks," Duncan told her, getting to his feet. "I've got to be going. I'm going to try to set something up with Robin and the Hoods."

"What do you mean?" Chrissy asked as Duncan started back over the wall.

"They're all Edmond High alums, you know. I thought I'd get a couple of informal shots of them rehearsing to go with the more formal performance pictures. Well, see you later," he said. Then he trotted off, leaving Chrissy staring after him.

Beth shook her head as she poured some ketchup onto her fries. "Why didn't you just tell him about you and the band just now? I mean, he's going to find out anyway, right?"

"I'm not rehearsing again with the band until Wednesday," Chrissy said. She peeled the paper wrapper off her straw and stuck it in her soda. "I guess I'll have told him by then anyway." As Chrissy took a sip, she smiled. "Can you imagine how surprised he's going to be when he sees me at Robin's Wednesday night?"

"I guess. I wonder who he's asking to the dance. Do you suppose he's thinking of asking you, Chrissy?"

"Didn't I tell you? He already did." Chrissy took a fry and dragged it through the ketchup on Beth's plate. "Of course, I told him I couldn't go with him."

"Why not? What's wrong with Duncan?"

"Nothing," Chrissy assured her. "I like Duncan."

"And he obviously likes you," Beth pointed out.

Chrissy shrugged. "I guess I know him too well. There's something so mysterious about Robin, and that's exciting."

"Yeah, but not when he's being mysterious

about whether or not he likes you. Besides, Duncan's taller than Robin," Beth argued.

"I'm not worried about height anymore. Duncan's better off dating some other girl. Can you imagine how awful our parents would be if we became more than friends all of a sudden?"

"They'd be thrilled!" Beth said, laughing.

Chrissy rolled her eyes. "That's exactly what I'm talking about!" she said, jabbing a french fry in the ketchup. "Wouldn't that be awful!"

Chapter Eleven

There were so many cars parked in Robin's driveway by the time Chrissy arrived Wednesday evening that she had to park on the street, several houses down from the Jameses' house.

After tiptoeing carefully through the new-fallen snow on Robin's driveway, Chrissy rang the back doorbell. Despite the care she'd taken not to get her feet wet, she could tell that some snow had gotten into her black flats anyway.

"Hi," Robin said as he opened the door. He sounded a little distracted. "Come on in! We're going to have a few people listening to us again tonight. Some guy from the high school's going to be taking pictures, too. Don't let all the commotion bother you."

Chrissy nodded. But it wasn't herself she was worried about. She had already seen how Robin acted when he felt pressured, and she wasn't anxious for a repeat performance. Then again, Robin had been so reasonable about the whole thing later that Chrissy told herself she had nothing to worry about. It wasn't going to happen again.

She followed Robin downstairs, half-afraid of seeing Duncan. Gary, Van, and Dave were clustered around Van's keyboard as usual.

"Chrissy's here!" Robin announced with a flourish as she stepped down the last few stairs.

"Chrissy!"

At the sound of Duncan's voice, Chrissy slowly turned, expecting to see his mouth hanging open in surprise. But when their eyes met, Chrissy saw that familiar, mischievous twinkle in Duncan's eyes. He wasn't at all surprised to see her there!

"Do you know Duncan West?" Robin asked.

Chrissy nodded. "We're old friends."

Chrissy was blinded by Duncan's flash. "Gotcha!" he cried. Then, lowering his camera so his green eyes were visible again, Duncan added, "That white leather jacket is wild with all that black. Is it new?"

Chrissy nodded. Duncan had noticed her outfit right away. *Why hadn't Robin?* she wondered. She had bought it especially because she thought he'd like it.

Chrissy turned to see if Duncan's comment had opened Robin's eyes any, but while Duncan had taken Chrissy's picture, he had moved away. He was now talking to a petite girl Chrissy recognized as an Edmond High graduate. The girl was wearing a miniskirt and above-the-knee suede boots. The delicate girl was a lot shorter than Robin. Chrissy couldn't help feeling jealous of both the other girl's size and the attention Robin was giving her.

"I bet you bought that jacket Monday, didn't you? That's what you had in that Beverly Eden bag I caught you with," Duncan said. "And you thought you were putting one over on me, didn't you?" He laughed.

Chrissy couldn't help feeling slighted by the way Robin ignored her whenever she got more attention than he did. Why couldn't he understand that she and Duncan were just friends, and that she wasn't trying to steal the spotlight? She couldn't help it if people liked her.

"Chrissy?" Duncan said, touching her arm. "Is something wrong?"

"Wrong?" Chrissy repeated. She had to force herself to look away from Robin and the girl he was so obviously flirting with. "Nothing's wrong. You just caught me off guard, that's all."

"I'll bet you thought I didn't know about your involvement with the band when I dropped my bombshell at the mall Monday, did you?" Duncan chuckled. "But I've known what you were up to for almost as long as you've been up to it."

Chrissy scowled. "How?" she demanded.

"Hey, that's privileged information! Remember, I'm a newsman. We never divulge our sources. Anyway, I figured if you weren't telling me, you had your reasons, so I didn't bug you. Then I got assigned to the Heartthrob Hop, so I thought I'd better warn you that I knew your little secret sooner than you wanted me to. You aren't mad, are you?"

Before Chrissy could answer, she heard Robin call her over.

"Better go," Duncan said. "We can talk about this more later if you want to."

"Everyone, this is Chrissy McCall," Robin said as soon as she was standing next to him. Even though Robin was wearing his boots and she was wearing her flats, Chrissy still *felt* that she was taller.

Robin slipped an arm around her. "Chrissy writes songs. We're going to play a couple of them tonight for you." Robin waved a finger in Duncan's direction. "Duncan over there is going to take some pictures of us rehearsing. So don't bother him or get in his way. Otherwise, we want you to have a good time and enjoy our music."

He dropped the hand that had been resting on Chrissy's waist. "Ready, Chrissy?" She nodded. "Ready, gang?" he called over his shoulder.

Gary played a quick drum roll and everyone laughed.

"Guess that means yes," Robin quipped as he strapped on his electric guitar.

The first song they sang was "Meant to Be." As their voices merged, Chrissy felt the same magic she'd felt before. All of Robin's attention was on her as they shared the chorus. Chrissy was vaguely aware of Duncan's flash, but she was too absorbed by the emotional song to let it distract her. When Robin sang the third verse, she knew he was singing to her and her alone.

But as soon as the song was over and the audience applauded their effort, Robin acted as if Chrissy were no more important to him than any of the other Hoods. Dumping his guitar in its stand, he hopped into the crowd and began talking to the short girl in the miniskirt again.

"That was great," Duncan said, giving Chrissy a quick hug.

"Thanks," she said softly.

"I mean it. You're as good as Angelina any day," Duncan told her. "In fact, you're better."

"You're just trying to make me feel better," Chrissy said dispiritedly.

"Better than what?" Duncan asked. He sounded confused. Obviously, he didn't understand how she felt about Robin. But how could he? Chrissy wasn't even sure how *she* felt about Robin anymore. She knew she wanted to perform with him in the band, but she still wanted more than that from him, didn't she?

Chrissy laughed nervously. "Oh, nothing. Forget it. I guess I just have preperformance jitters or something."

Duncan nodded as if he understood. But Chrissy could tell that he didn't know the real reason for her bad mood, and she was glad.

Robin tapped her on the shoulder. "Come on, Chrissy. We're on again. We do have work to do, you know."

Chrissy joined Robin again, and this time they sang "Hello, Stranger." As they sang, Chrissy felt almost as if she were saying goodbye to him. She still wanted to perform with him, but they were never going to be anything more than friends. It had nothing to do with height, either. Robin was too self-centered for her. He wanted top billing. Anything less than that threatened his ego, the part of him that Chrissy now knew was the smallest thing about him. Even two-inch heels on his boots wouldn't correct that particular shortcoming.

When they'd finished running through "Hello, Stranger" a couple of times, Robin announced a break, after which the band was going to get down to some serious rehearsing. Once again, he seemed to have time for just about everyone in the room except Chrissy and, of course,

Gary, Van, and Dave. Robin was the star, he seemed to be saying with his behavior. The Hoods were just his backup. He wanted them to stay in the shadows.

Chrissy grabbed a can of diet soda and talked with Dave for a while about his bass. He let her try it out, showing her some fairly uncomplicated fingering. Chrissy did her best to ignore Robin. But it was hard. He seemed to be so totally tuned in to her while they were singing together that it was almost painful to see the feelings disappear when the music ended.

A little while later, as Robin clowned around a bit on Van's keyboard, Chrissy began edging toward the stairs. Even though it was only a little after ten and she didn't have to be home until eleven, she'd decided it was time to leave.

Just as her foot slowly touched the bottom stair, a camera flashed nearby. "Sneaking out?" Duncan asked as the automatic film rewinder in his camera whirred away.

Chrissy put her finger to her lips and nodded.

Duncan smiled. "Good. I'll sneak out with you."

Chrissy shook her head. "You don't have to do that. I've got my own car and everything tonight. Besides, you're not finished here, are you?"

"I am if you are. Without you, the band isn't nearly as interesting."

"Shh!" she commanded with a scowl. "Don't let Robin hear you say something like that. He'll flip."

"Then we better get out of here while he's busy over there. Lead the way, Chrissy."

When they were finally out in the crisp night air, Chrissy felt as if she had escaped.

"How about grabbing that pizza we never got to have last week?" Duncan suggested.

"Your apology pizza?" she said with a laugh.

Duncan nodded. "Only now it'll be a celebration pizza. To you, Chrissy, and the beginning of your rise to the top."

"But we've got two cars," she reminded him.

"So? We'll just meet at Pied Piper Pizza then. Last one there is a rotten egg!" he added, taking off like a flash, despite the two cameras hanging around his neck.

Chrissy tried to hurry, but her black flats slipped on the icy driveway and she fell down on her rear end with a thud. Duncan had reached the Green Pea by the time she fell, but he turned around and jogged back.

"Are you all right?" he asked, bending down to help her up.

"Aren't you going to take a picture of me, sprawled on the ground like this? You could use it in the *Buzzette* next week," Chrissy said, slyly gathering a handful of snow in her left hand.

Duncan looked away and blushed. "I don't mean to embarrass you. I only take so many pictures of you because I—"

Chrissy jumped up off the ground and stuffed the snow in the neck of Duncan's brown bomber jacket. "Because you're cold!" she yelled.

"Hey!" Duncan yelped.

"Better hurry," she taunted him as she opened the door of her father's Chevy. "Last one there is a rotten anchovy!"

Chapter Twelve

"Hi," Chrissy said, setting her lunch tray on the table.

"There you are!" Beth cried. "I was worried about you when you didn't get on the bus this morning. How did things go at Robin's last night?"

"Everything was great. I just overslept this morning, that's all. Mom had to drive me to school," Chrissy said. Then she added dreamily, "Oh, Beth, he's so wonderful. I mean, I guess I knew that before. But then I didn't really know. Do you know what I'm saying?"

"Of course. You're saying you're in love," Beth replied.

"That's right." Chrissy nodded enthusiastically. "I just can't believe it. I'm in love! Really in love."

"I know, I know. You've been raving about

Robin James ever since we heard Robin and the Hoods at River Fest." Beth speared a lettuce leaf and popped it into her mouth. "So what's the latest? Did he finally kiss you?"

Chrissy shook her head. "I'm not talking about Robin, silly."

Beth started choking and had to take a quick drink of water. "What did you say?" she demanded.

"I said, I'm not in love with Robin James. I guess I never really was. He's a good musician and everything. I really like singing with him. But he's not my type. At least, not romantically."

"Is this change of heart because he's too short?" Beth asked cautiously.

Chrissy nodded. "You could say that, but not in the way you think. Actually, his height has nothing to do with this."

"I have no idea what you're talking about," Beth told her honestly.

Chrissy couldn't help grinning. "You're not going to believe this."

Beth grinned. "Try me."

"I'm in love with Duncan West," Chrissy said. She looked expectantly at Beth, waiting for her to choke again. But Beth didn't look the least bit surprised.

"Aren't you going to say something?" She finally asked.

Beth shrugged. "What can I say, except, it's about time?"

"You're not surprised?"

"Hardly. But how did all this happen? What made you finally see the light?"

"I guess it was seeing Duncan at Robin's last night. Duncan is thoughtful and Robin is kind of self-centered. But Duncan's more than just thoughtful. He's fun, too. We went out for a pizza and . . ." Chrissy paused, searching for just the right words to describe her moment of revelation.

"You fell into each other's arms over the pepperoni, right?" Beth supplied.

Chrissy giggled. "Hardly. It was more subtle than that. I guess I finally realized how cute Duncan is, inside and out. I feel comfortable with myself when I'm with him."

Beth nodded. "That's how I feel when I'm with Paul. It's like being excited and calm at the same time."

"Uh-oh," Chrissy said. She nodded her head at the door to the cafeteria. "Here come Avis and Vicky. They look mad about something."

"They've probably discovered what you've been up to and are mad because you didn't tell them sooner," Beth guessed. "I know I'd be mad if you hadn't told me."

"Hi," Avis said coolly, setting her tray down

next to Chrissy's with a loud thud. "I just found out something very interesting. A girl from this high school, a member of our very own junior class, is playing her own original music with Robin and the Hoods at the dance on Saturday night." She gave Chrissy a piercing look. "Do you have any idea who that girl could be?"

"Yeah, Chrissy," Vicky seconded. She looked almost as put out as Avis. "It's all over school that you've been working with the band. Why didn't you tell us? I mean, I felt pretty dumb that everyone else knew what one of my best friends was up to before I did."

"I'm sorry," Chrissy said sheepishly. "I guess I was so nervous about the whole thing that I didn't want anyone to know about it. I was afraid it would bring me bad luck or something. You see, things were kind of up in the air until last night, really."

"But now that it's out in the open, isn't it great news?" Beth prompted.

"Sure, it's great," Avis reluctantly agreed. "I just wish Chrissy had trusted us, that's all."

"Oh, well," Beth said, "what's done is done. Right? The important thing is that all four of us will be going to the dance after all. And just think, we'll actually get to dance to Chrissy's music."

"Hey, that's right!" Vicky cried. Not one to

stay mad longer than five minutes at a stretch, she smiled at Chrissy. Avis would be a little slower to get over the feeling of being slighted, but thanks to Beth, she was already on her way. Chrissy returned Vicky's smile, then smiled hopefully at Avis.

As the conversation moved on to what everyone would be wearing to the dance and where they should all go afterward, Chrissy found her thoughts drifting to Duncan. He'd asked her to the dance once, and she'd turned him down. How could she get him to ask her again so that she could accept?

By the time lunch was over and Chrissy was on her way to her locker to get the books she needed for her afternoon classes, she knew what she had to do. She simply had to march up to Duncan and ask him to the dance herself. After all, he was planning on going anyway, and he'd practically said he needed a date who realized he couldn't spend every minute with her. It was going to work out perfectly because Chrissy wouldn't be able to spend every minute with him either.

Chrissy reached her locker and started dialing her combination. After she'd taken out everything she needed, she turned around to go to her next class, and suddenly she saw a familiar fedora bobbing along in the crowd.

"Duncan!" she yelled, hurrying after him. Now seemed like as good a time as any to ask him. She didn't really have any time to lose, since it was already Thursday.

But when Chrissy got closer to Duncan, she saw that he wasn't alone. There was a petite brunette with sparkling blue eyes walking with him. It only took a second more for Chrissy to realize that Duncan's arm was around her shoulder!

Shrinking back into the nearest doorway, Chrissy watched them laugh companionably as they walked down the hall. She wasn't the only one who had been keeping secrets. Duncan hadn't mentioned this girl to her, at least not that she could remember.

Once they were out of sight, Chrissy darted up the stairs to the second floor. If she didn't hurry, she'd be late to her next class. The crowd in the halls began to thin as everyone went into their rooms. Chrissy started to run. She wanted to keep running, too, right past her classroom, right out of the school building. She had waited too long to realize how she felt about Duncan, and now it was too late. He had found someone else!

"Good night, Mr. Levi," Chrissy mumbled over her shoulder as she left The Golden Note Thursday evening.

"Good night, Chrissy," her boss called after her. "Now you go right to bed. I don't think I've ever seen you have such little energy."

Chrissy nodded, shuffling out the door. It had been easier for Chrissy to let Mr. Levi go on thinking she was tired than to tell him that she was depressed. But she knew that was it. She could have gone to the dance with Duncan, but she'd blown it. She couldn't put that horrible thought out of her mind.

Chrissy walked outside, looking around to find her father's light-blue Chevy where it was usually parked in the loading zone. But instead of the Chevy, the Green Pea was there. She wanted to run to Duncan's car and throw her arms around his neck, but she held back, forcing herself to walk at a normal pace.

"Hi," she said softly as she climbed into the car. "This is a surprise."

"It shouldn't be too much of one," Duncan said as he put his car in gear. "You must have known that your parents are playing bridge with my parents tonight at our house."

"I guess I forgot," Chrissy admitted. She noticed that the palms of her hands had grown damp. Being with Duncan was actually making her nervous!

"So, when's your next rehearsal with the band?" Duncan asked. His tone was light and friendly.

"Tomorrow night, I guess." She cleared her throat nervously. "I haven't talked to Robin since we snuck out last night. I'll have to call him when I get home. I just hope he isn't mad."

"He can't really afford to be mad at you, can he? I mean, everyone at school knows that you're going to be singing with him Saturday night. It was the talk of the halls today." Suddenly, Duncan threw back his head and laughed.

"What's so funny?" Chrissy demanded as Duncan stopped for a red light.

"It's kind of a long story," he said.

"Tell me."

"Okay, if you insist. There's this sophomore girl who just moved up here from Iowa over winter break. Anyway, she's been putting a lot of pressure on Malcolm Daly, our editor, to let her join the *Buzzette* staff." Duncan shook his head. "Finally, last week she came up with this column called The Talk of the Halls that Malcolm went crazy for. Somehow, I keep unconsciously working that phrase into everything I say, like some sort of walking advertisement. Anyway, her column's going to debut in next week's edition."

"Oh?" Chrissy said nonchalantly. "What's this girl's name anyway? I don't think you ever said. Maybe I know her."

"Her name's Amy Gruber," Duncan said.

Chrissy couldn't help but notice that Duncan's eyes sparkled as he said the name. "She's a real dynamo, too, the kind of girl who refuses to take no for an answer. I really admire that quality."

"In a girl?" Chrissy asked. She had taken Duncan for granted for so long that now she'd begun to question exactly how well she really knew him.

"In anyone," he told her.

"What does Amy look like?" Chrissy pressed, although she was pretty certain she already knew.

"Let's see," Duncan said thoughtfully. "She has dark-brown hair, kind of short and curly, and she has really pretty blue eyes. She's fairly short."

"The best things come in small packages," Chrissy mumbled.

"What did you say?" Duncan asked, glancing at her as he paused briefly for a stop sign.

"Oh, nothing," Chrissy said with a sigh. "I guess I don't know who she is."

Duncan turned the car up the McCalls' driveway. "I can fix that. I'll introduce you to each other at the dance. I'm sure you'll like her as much as I do."

"At the dance?" Chrissy repeated just as Duncan came to a stop at the top of the driveway.

"Well, sure. Is there anything wrong with that?"

"Oh, no," Chrissy said, reaching for the door handle. "Well, bye. And thanks for the ride."

Duncan smiled. "Sure, Chrissy. Anytime."

But as she jogged up to the empty house and let herself in, Chrissy couldn't help wondering how much longer that would be true. It was pretty clear that Duncan was in love . . . and not with her!

Chapter Thirteen

"Now that you've seen them together with your own eyes, what do you think, Beth?" Chrissy asked, sinking back against her locker. "Do you think it's hopeless? Or do you think I still have a chance?"

"It's hardly hopeless," Beth assured her calmly. "Look, the dance is tomorrow night, right?"

Chrissy nodded. "So?"

"So, you'll be at the dance; they'll be at the dance. At some point, you'll catch Duncan and Amy. You'll ask him to dance. While you're out on the dance floor in each other's arms, he'll see the light."

Chrissy rolled her eyes. "Get real, Beth. You've been watching too many soap operas."

Beth shrugged. "Maybe I have. But I think things like that can happen. You just have to help them along, that's all. Come on, or we'll miss our bus," she added. She started walking down the hall, and Chrissy fell in step with her.

"Well, I don't think just dancing with Duncan is going to be enough. You saw for yourself the way he looks at her."

"Not really," Beth told her as the girls boarded the bus. "All I saw was Duncan and a short girl with curly hair laughing about something. He wasn't looking at her in any special way that I could see."

"When people of the opposite sex laugh with each other like that it's called flirting," Chrissy said. The bus began to roll out of the loading area in front of the school, and Chrissy had to grip the seat in front of her to keep from falling into the aisle.

"Maybe they are interested in each other," Beth conceded. "But if they are, it's just the beginning stages."

"Love is at its most intense in the beginning stages," Chrissy announced gloomily.

Beth shook her head. "You've really got a case, haven't you? I think you just *want* to feel bad. I don't know why I'm even bothering to try to cheer you up."

Chrissy nodded. "I deserve to feel miserable. I could have had it all! What a dope I've been."

"Okay, now. Let's be reasonable about this," Beth said, sounding more patient. "You said you talked to Duncan about Amy last night when he gave you a ride home from work, right?"

Chrissy nodded. She felt as if she were going to cry.

"He didn't actually say he was in love with her, did he?" Beth pointed out.

"He didn't *have* to say he was in love. It was written all over his face. He told me he *admires* Amy, for Pete's sake! How much more can a person say than that?" Chrissy demanded.

"Admiration and love aren't the same thing," Beth said. "But I'm not going to argue with you about it anymore."

Chrissy sighed as she looked out the window at the passing scenery. All the white snow made the town of Edmond Heights look desolate. "Well, don't get mad."

"I'm not mad. You're the one who sounds mad."

"You're right. I am, but not at you," Chrissy admitted. "I'm mad at me. I thought my dreams were finally coming true and now . . ."

Beth gave Chrissy a sympathetic look. "Some of your dreams *are* coming true. Don't forget you're still doing your songs with the band at the Heartthrob Hop."

"Right," Chrissy scoffed. " 'Heartache' Hop is more like it! I mean, how can I stand up on that stage singing love songs when the boy I love is right in front of me, with his arms around another girl? It's a nightmare, Beth."

Beth shrugged. "Nightmares are dreams, too, you know."

"Wow!" Chrissy cried, giving Beth an amazed look. "Quick. Give me a sheet of paper."

"Another song?" Beth asked, hurrying to provide Chrissy with a piece of paper.

Chrissy nodded as she took the paper and put it on top of her books. "You just came up with a great line for a song. 'Nightmares are dreams, too,'" Chrissy repeated as she opened her shoulder bag and dug around until she'd found a pen. "Can I use it?" she asked, scrawling the phrase on the paper.

"Of course," Beth agreed. "Be my guest."

Chrissy stared down at Beth's words for a minute, then she quickly added:

> Nightmares, nightmares
> Nightmares are dreams, too,
> and just like dreams they can come true.
> Every night I dreamt
> of losing you
> Now here you are to tell me we're through.

Beth looked over Chrissy's shoulder while she wrote. "Wow! I really like that. How does the melody go?" she asked.

Chrissy shrugged. "I don't know yet. I'll have

to work on that when I get home. Probably a minor key. You know, really sad sounding."

"Do I get to be the first one to hear it?" Beth asked as the bus neared her stop.

"You might be the *only* one to hear it," Chrissy warned her.

"What about Robin?" Beth asked.

"What about Robin?" Chrissy replied. "It's hard to know from one minute to the next *what* kind of a mood he'll be in."

"Well, what time do you have to be at his house tonight for rehearsal?" Beth asked as she stood up to get off the bus.

"He said anytime between seven and eight."

"Can I come with you?"

"Would you? That would be great! Want me to pick you up then?"

Beth shook her head. "Paul and I will pick you up a little after seven."

Chrissy smiled. Just knowing that her best friend would be there to give her moral support made everything seem better.

"Hi," Beth said as Chrissy climbed into the backseat of Paul's Toyota and slammed the door. "I hope we're not late."

"Robin says there's no such thing as late," Chrissy told her. She placed her guitar case on the seat next to her, then fastened her seat belt.

"I've never been to a band rehearsal before," Paul told her. "This will be great."

"I'm glad you could come. This is the last rehearsal before the big dance, and I'm starting to get a little nervous," Chrissy confessed.

"You'll be great tonight—and tomorrow night, too," Beth assured her with a smile as Paul pulled out of the McCalls' driveway. "Wait until you hear her, Paul. Chrissy's as good or even better than anything on the radio."

"Come on, Beth," Chrissy pleaded.

"I wouldn't say it if I didn't mean it. I'd think you were terrific even if you weren't my best friend," Beth insisted.

"Well, I'm convinced, and I haven't even heard a note yet," Paul said. Looking over his shoulder, he gave Chrissy an encouraging smile.

There weren't very many cars parked outside Robin's house, and as they walked up to the back door and rang the bell, Chrissy worried that Robin might be less than thrilled to see she'd brought a couple of her friends along. But luckily, he seemed to be in a good mood.

"Come in, come in!" he said cheerfully after Chrissy had introduced everyone. "It's all happening downstairs."

Once they reached the basement, Robin graciously showed Paul and Beth around. He even offered them each a can of soda. Then he joined Chrissy and the rest of the band.

"We've been working here all afternoon," Robin told Chrissy as he strapped on his guitar. "We'll run through your stuff now. Then we're heading out to Ricky's Diner for burgers and fries. I hope you three will come, too."

Chrissy nodded. "That sounds like a good time. I'll ask Beth and Paul about it."

As always, something clicked when Chrissy and Robin started singing together. But as exciting as singing with Robin was, Chrissy knew she had her feelings for him under control, and she was glad. It meant she was closer to being the professional she wanted to be.

"Shall we run through it again?" she asked after the last chord had faded out. Now that they were cooking, she was reluctant to have their rehearsal end. She felt as if she could continue playing all night.

But Robin shook his head. "Let's call it a night. I'm starved."

Chrissy grinned. "Now that you mention it, I'm kind of hungry myself."

"Okay, everyone. It's a wrap. The Hoodmobile leaves for Ricky's in ten minutes." Robin unstrapped his guitar and placed it in its metal holder.

Twenty minutes later, Paul was pulling into the parking lot at Ricky's Diner, an old railway car that had been converted into a restaurant.

Chrissy got out of the car and was heading

over to the van to join the guys when a car suddenly swerved in front of her. Chrissy jumped back out of the way and glared at the careless driver. Then she saw that it was Duncan!

"Hey, Chrissy!" Duncan yelled out the window of the Green Pea. "Are you coming or going?"

"Coming," Robin replied, stepping up next to Chrissy. He gave Duncan a brief nod. "Want to join us? We're feeling photogenic tonight. Aren't we, Chrissy?" He put his arm across her shoulders and gave her a squeeze.

"Sure," Chrissy agreed cheerfully, despite the fact that she'd just spotted Amy in the car with Duncan.

Duncan lifted the camera that was hanging around his neck to show them that he was prepared as usual.

"We'll go in and grab a booth," Robin told him. "Meet us inside," he added in his typical take-charge tone of voice.

The bright chrome interior of the diner and the warm rush of fragrant air that greeted her as she stepped inside made Chrissy wonder why she didn't come here more often. Working at the mall so many hours a week, she had let herself slide into a rut. Being with the band was definitely expanding her horizons.

"Hi, Robin," a waitress wearing a name tag

that said "Shirley" greeted him. "Your favorite booth in the back is open."

"See? It pays to be a regular," Robin said. He motioned for the others to follow him to the back of the long, narrow diner.

The booth was curved along the back, making it the largest table in the place. Still, there wasn't quite enough room for everyone.

Taking hold of Chrissy's elbow, Robin herded her toward a booth nearby. "Chrissy and I will sit over here," he directed over his shoulder to the others. He motioned for Beth and Paul to join Chrissy and himself. "Duncan can sit with us, too," he added. "It'll be tight, but we'll manage."

"Here they come now," Beth announced as she slid into the booth across from Robin and Chrissy. "Hi, Duncan."

"Hi, everyone. This is Amy Gruber," Duncan said, squeezing in next to Paul. "Amy is the *Buzzette*'s newest reporter."

Amy smiled admiringly at Duncan. "Duncan's sort of taken me under his wing. I guess you could say he's my mentor."

"Were you two at the game?" Paul asked once Duncan had finished introducing everyone to Amy. "Who won?"

"We did, of course," Duncan answered. "The Hornets have the conference title sewn up now."

"It was a great game," Amy concurred.

"I discovered tonight that Amy's a basketball connoisseur," Duncan announced. "She really understands the fine points of the game."

Amy laughed. "I have three older brothers," she explained.

"I wish I'd seen the game." Paul sounded wistful. Then he glanced at Beth and quickly added, "But no one can be two places at once, right?"

"Right," Beth agreed evenly.

"You can still see the game," Amy promised Paul. "Duncan got some wonderful pictures that will be on next week's sports page." Amy patted the back of Duncan's hand. Then she asked, "What have you all been up to? Is this the tail end of a party?"

Robin laughed. "You might say that."

"Actually, we've been rehearsing," Chrissy told her.

"Chrissy is the songwriter I was telling you about," Duncan explained.

"Of course!" Amy cried, rapping her forehead with the heel of her hand. "How dumb of me. *You're* the Chrissy Duncan's always talking about."

"What'll it be?" Shirley asked, cutting into the conversation. She was tapping her pencil impatiently on her order pad and swaying to the rock 'n' roll song that was playing on the jukebox.

"I'll have the burger basket and a chocolate malt," Chrissy told her.

Paul and Beth ordered next, then Robin. Just as Duncan was about to order, a loud commotion at the door made everyone turn to check it out.

"It's the team!" Amy squealed joyfully. "You were right, Duncan. You said they were coming here. Do you think they'll let me interview them?" she asked, already on her feet.

Duncan chuckled. "How could anyone possibly say no to you?" he teased her.

"Are you coming with me?" Amy asked eagerly.

"Of course," Duncan replied, edging out of the booth after her. "You'll need pictures, won't you?"

"It was nice meeting you all," Amy said absently, her attention clearly focused on the basketball team.

As she watched Amy and Duncan cross to the other side of the diner, Chrissy sighed with relief. Having to sit with the pair of them while they exchanged admiring comments had been a little too much for her to take!

"Hey, how about another tune?" Paul asked. He pulled a quarter from the pocket of his jeans. "Any special requests?" he asked, waving the coin at them.

"How about something by Angelina?" Beth

asked, looking at Chrissy sympathetically. "She's Chrissy's favorite."

Paul flipped through the selections. "Here's 'I'm Your Girl.' Isn't that number one this week?"

"How about something else?" Chrissy suggested. She liked the song so much that she was afraid hearing it now would only make her more sad.

"I thought that was your favorite song," Beth said.

Chrissy shrugged. "I guess I'm just tired of it, that's all," she said, stealing a quick look in Duncan's direction.

What she saw surprised her. Amy was talking animatedly with Jeff Henderson while Duncan stared absently off into space, fiddling with his camera.

Shirley set a huge plate of fries in front of Chrissy. She dragged a hot, crispy fry through the ketchup, then looked back across the diner.

Duncan looked totally left out, despite the fact that he was snapping a few pictures of the players. Amy was chatting away with Jeff and didn't seem to notice that she was ignoring her date. *Duncan deserves more from a girl than what Amy's giving him*, Chrissy fumed to herself.

Then, all at once, her mind was buzzing with new song lyrics. *If I was your girl, you'd be all*

I'd see. If I was with you, that would be enough for me.

Dropping her half-eaten fry, Chrissy grabbed her shoulder bag and pulled out a pencil. While everyone around her talked about the Heartthrob Hop, she took a paper napkin out of the dispenser and started writing down the lyrics.

"Chrissy? Did you hear me?"

Chrissy looked up and saw Robin, Beth, and Paul staring at her expectantly.

"I'm sorry," Chrissy said, feeling her cheeks color. "Did you ask me something, Robin?"

Robin nodded. "I asked if you thought a drum solo would be too much for 'Meant to Be.' You know, sort of overwhelm it, like that tune that was just on the box?" Robin said cautiously.

"I wasn't really listening," Chrissy admitted.

"You were writing a song, weren't you?" Beth demanded eagerly. "That's how Chrissy writes her songs, you know," she told the boys. "She'll just be sitting somewhere and an idea comes to her and she's got to write it right down."

"No, I didn't know. Are you really writing a song right now, Chrissy?" Robin peered at the paper napkin lying under Chrissy's hand.

"I was," she confessed. "But I didn't get it down fast enough." She balled up the napkin and stuffed it in her pocket.

"Maybe it'll come back to you," Beth offered encouragingly.

"Maybe," Chrissy agreed. She chucked the pencil back into her purse. The song itself didn't matter anyway. What mattered was that Chrissy had just realized she had a chance of getting Duncan back. She was going to do it at the dance, too, but not quite the way Beth had suggested. She couldn't wait to put her plan into action!

Chapter Fourteen

"Don't forget to ask Duncan for a copy of the best picture he gets of you up on stage tonight," Mrs. McCall called as Chrissy hurried out to the Hoodmobile Saturday night.

"Sure, Mom," Chrissy yelled over her shoulder just before she slammed the front door. She was glad her parents were as excited about her performance as she was. They hadn't been pleased to find out she'd been hiding something from them, but they realized how important her first shot at becoming a professional singer was to her, and why she had kept it a secret at first.

"Hey, Chrissy!" the guys cried in a chorus as they helped her into the back of the van.

"There's a box of cassette tapes under the seat," Robin told her as she settled in between Van and Gary. "Why don't you look through them for some music you like?" He looked back over his shoulder at her and smiled. "Find something that'll get us all in the mood for this gig."

Chrissy pulled out the tape box and put it on her lap. She was grateful for something to do. She was feeling nervous—and not just about playing with the band, either.

"Any requests?" she asked as she sifted through the large assortment.

"Anything in there would be fine," Robin assured her.

Looking over Chrissy's shoulder, Gary tapped a cassette. "How about this group? I like a lot of sound, you know, the kind you can actually feel here." He patted his chest, and Chrissy shuddered. Heavy metal definitely left her cold! But if she was going to fit in with the band, she was going to have to make concessions.

"Okay," she agreed, pulling the tape out and handing it to Robin.

"One of these days I'm going to switch from tape to CD sound in here," Robin said as he popped the cassette into his player. The music that filled the van was so loud that it precluded any more discussion. But it served its purpose. Chrissy felt herself relax and also get excited so that by the time they reached the high school, she was ready.

While the group unloaded their equipment to carry into the cafeteria, Chrissy excused herself and darted into the ladies' room for a quick makeup check. She'd worn more makeup than usual and she wanted to make sure it looked all right. Chrissy was trying to decide if she needed more hot-pink lipstick when Amy walked into the room.

"Hi. Are you nervous?" Amy asked Chrissy. She looked as if she was taking mental notes for her new column.

"A little," Chrissy admitted warily. "What are you doing here so early?"

Amy rolled her eyes. "You know Duncan! He wanted to take some pictures of the band setting up. Hey, I really like that jacket. I saw one just like it at Beverly Eden, but it was miles too big for me."

Chrissy couldn't help laughing. "It was probably this very one. I got it at Beverly Eden and I'm miles bigger than you are."

Amy shook her head. "You're so lucky you're tall, Chrissy. It's really hard to find anything decent to wear when you're a pip-squeak like me."

"You're hardly a pip-squeak," Chrissy insisted, amazed that Amy didn't seem happy with what Chrissy considered her perfect size. Then she added, "Believe me, being tall is no picnic. Boys are really self-conscious about going out with girls who are taller than they are."

"All the guys on the basketball team are taller

than you are," Amy said wistfully. She tossed her comb back into her bag. "Some of them are too tall to take a shorty like me seriously, that's for sure."

Chrissy shrugged, a little annoyed. It almost seemed as if Amy were encouraging her to go after a basketball player and forget about Duncan. "I'm not really into basketball," she said.

Amy shook her head and laughed. "Isn't that just the way it goes?" she asked. But before Chrissy could ask what she meant by that, there was a loud knock on the rest-room door.

"You in there, Chrissy? We need you now for a sound check," Dave called.

"Coming!" Chrissy yelled back.

"You look great," Amy assured her as Chrissy gave her makeup one last careful check.

"Thanks. See you later," she told Amy.

As Chrissy entered the cafeteria, she saw Van scurrying around, plugging in the various amps. Dave and Gary were huddled over the mixer, and Chrissy went over to join them. "Hi, guys. What do you want me to do?"

"Find Robin and sing. We need to check the sound levels," Dave told her.

"No need to find me," Robin said, sliding up next to Chrissy, " 'cause here I am." Robin looked Chrissy up and down and whistled. "You look great!"

"This is the same outfit I wore at rehearsal the other night," Chrissy pointed out.

"I get so tense at rehearsals that I usually don't notice much of anything," Robin admitted. "Anyway, that jacket definitely makes you fit right in with the rest of the Hoods. You won't worry about having to find a costume. I guess all you have to worry about now is getting that electric guitar you've been saving for."

"Robin!" Chrissy cried. "Are you saying what I think you're saying?"

"That depends on what you think I'm saying," Robin teased, raising one dark eyebrow.

"Are you saying you're making me an official member of the band?" she asked, her voice barely louder than a whisper.

Robin nodded. "We took a vote last night. It was unanimous. We need you, Chrissy. I think this band's getting ready to really take off. Your songs have given us the wings we'd been missing."

"Oh, Robin!" Chrissy cried, throwing her arms around him and giving him an impulsive hug. "I'm so happy!"

"Hold that pose!" Duncan commanded. Then there was a flash. He had caught Robin and Chrissy locked in an embrace! Realizing how their hug must look, Chrissy quickly dropped her arms and stepped back.

"Hi," she said, noticing that Duncan was wearing the same familiar dark-green corduroy jacket that she'd always liked, and a pair of khaki pants. His fedora was perched on his head at a rakish angle. He looked adorable.

"Chrissy! Robin!" Van called over to them before Chrissy could say anything else to Duncan. "Get on up here, will you? We've still got to check out the mikes and people are starting to arrive." There was a squeal from one of the mammoth speakers, and Chrissy jumped.

"Better get used to that," Robin warned. "It sort of comes with the territory."

Chrissy nodded. She turned back to say goodbye to Duncan, but he'd already wandered away.

Gary and Dave materialized, and the four of them started to play a few notes and sing a bit while Van fine-tuned the sound levels. Chrissy knew she had to put her feelings for Duncan on hold for a minute and concentrate on her performance. This was what she'd been working so hard for. And soon the cafeteria would be crowded and the dance would begin.

"That's it," Van finally announced. "We're ready to roll."

"You can stay up here if you want, Chrissy," Robin offered. "We're going to do a couple of songs, though, before we officially introduce you."

"I guess I'll wander around a little then. I'd like to find my friends and say hello before I go on," she said, thinking of Duncan.

"Don't get too far away," Robin cautioned her.

"Don't worry, I won't," Chrissy assured him. She headed for the refreshment table, where she had seen Duncan earlier.

"Chrissy!" she heard Beth call as she reached for a glass of punch.

Turning, she saw Beth, Avis, and Vicky with their dates. "Hi," she said, waving them over.

"Oooh!" Vicky exclaimed. "I love that white leather jacket, Chrissy."

"Thanks," Chrissy told her.

"When are you going to sing?" Beth asked.

"Soon," Chrissy answered. She took a deep breath. "*Very* soon. Did you just get here?"

Beth nodded. "Just this second." She smiled at Paul.

"Come on, Avis. Let's dance," Mike said, pulling her out into the crowd.

"Good luck, Chrissy," Avis called over her shoulder.

"Mike's got the right idea. Let's dance, Vicky," Dave Mullen said. "After all, it's what we're here for."

"How about it, Beth?" Paul asked. "Want to dance?"

"Would you mind, Chrissy?" Beth asked, holding back. "We could wait with you until it's time for you to go on."

"Of course I don't mind," Chrissy said, trying not to sound eager to get rid of her best friend.

She needed to see Duncan alone before she went on, though, or her plan was never going to get off the ground. "Dance. I'll see you later."

Beth smiled. "Definitely!" She gave Chrissy a hug. "And good luck!"

After Beth and Paul danced away, Chrissy began scanning the crowd for Duncan. She couldn't see him anywhere, though. She told herself it was just as well. He was probably dancing with Amy anyway.

Chrissy sighed. Maybe she'd been wrong to think that Amy and Duncan didn't belong together just because Amy didn't seem to devote enough time to Duncan. No girl could devote herself entirely to a guy. No guy would probably want her to, anyway—at least, Duncan wouldn't. That was what was so special about him. He had always encouraged her to go after whatever it was she wanted. He had always been so supportive.

Suddenly, Chrissy felt a hand on her shoulder and spun around.

"Looking for someone?" Duncan asked.

"Hi," she said, smiling with relief. "I was looking for you. My parents wanted to be sure you knew they wanted a copy of your best picture. You know, of me on stage with the guys." Then she noticed that he was alone.

"Where's your date?" she asked.

"My date?" Duncan frowned.

"Amy," Chrissy prompted.

Duncan laughed. "Oh, she's with Jeff Henderson." He nodded at the dance floor, where Chrissy spotted Jeff in the middle of the crowd. "She's convinced he's going to be voted Hero of the Hop tonight and she thought that if she danced with him, she might get an exclusive for her new column."

"I thought she interviewed him last night," Chrissy said, unable to hide the disapproval in her voice. Dancing with Jeff when Amy was Duncan's date was a little too rude, Chrissy thought.

"A little bit, I guess, but that was about the basketball game. I don't think they're talking about basketball tonight. You see, Amy has this thing about tall guys in general and basketball players in particular." Duncan's playful wink surprised Chrissy.

"You mean, she's out there *flirting* with Jeff?" Chrissy exclaimed.

"I guess the word 'flirting' is as good a word as any," Duncan said thoughtfully. Then he added, "Yes, I'd have to say that's about the *long* and *short* of it." He gave Chrissy a playful jab in the rib cage with his elbow. "If you get my meaning."

Just then Amy and Jeff came dancing into view and Chrissy had to laugh. Jeff was about a foot and a half taller than Amy. The two of them did look kind of silly together.

"But who are we to judge?" Duncan said philosophically. He looked as if he were trying hard not to laugh.

"Aren't you jealous?" Chrissy asked as Amy danced right by without acknowledging Duncan, her eyes focused dreamily on Jeff.

"Why would I be jealous?"

"I thought you and Amy . . . I mean, I thought you two were . . ."

Duncan stared hard at Chrissy. "We're just working together, that's all. What did you think?"

Chrissy could feel her heart pounding and she tried to wipe the silly grin off her face. "Just friends?" she asked hopefully.

Duncan nodded. "Unlike you and Robin James," he said pensively.

"Me and Robin James?" Chrissy repeated.

"I have eyes. I saw the two of you hugging. In fact, I captured it on film, if you remember."

"You might have eyes, but I don't think you have ears," Chrissy quipped. "Because if you did, you'd know *why* I hugged him. Robin asked me to join the band—permanently! I'm a Hood!" she exclaimed excitedly. "Or at least, I will be."

"Hey, Chrissy!" Duncan cried, throwing his arms around her. "That's—"

"Ouch!" Chrissy cried out as Duncan crushed her against his camera.

Duncan drew back a little but he didn't let

Chrissy go. "I guess I'll have to do something about this camera," he said. "It's come between us once too often, don't you think?"

Chrissy nodded. "That's for sure."

Suddenly, the band's second song ended. "Chrissy?" Robin's voice boomed out of the speakers. "Where are you, luv?"

"Love?" Duncan said, narrowing his green eyes at Chrissy suspiciously.

"It's just a figure of speech." Chrissy gave him an impish grin. "You know, part of the British influence on rock . . . Robin and I are just friends, like you and Amy are, I guess. I've got to go," she told Duncan, slipping out of his arms and starting toward the stage. "But I'll be back."

"I'll be waiting," Duncan assured her.

Chrissy had almost reached the stage when she felt someone put something on her head. When she reached up, she touched felt.

Turning back, she said, "Oh, Duncan. Your hat!"

He gave her a two-fingered salute. "It's just a loan. For luck," he said. "Not that you really need it."

Chrissy gathered her long hair in her hand and tossed it over one shoulder, then adjusted the hat on her head. "How does it look?"

But instead of answering her question with words, Duncan gave Chrissy a quick kiss. Then he slipped back into the crowd.

Seconds later, Chrissy was on stage, strapping on her old acoustic guitar. The crowd went wild after Robin introduced her as the writer of the songs they were about to hear. Then the intro began and Robin and Chrissy started singing the first verse of "Meant to Be."

When they reached Chrissy's solo, she gazed out into the crowd, looking for Duncan. She smiled at him, then sang, "Hey, boy! Are we meant to be? I want you to know that I think so. Hey, boy!"

When the song ended, the crowd went wild. Duncan gave Chrissy the thumbs-up signal before he snapped a quick picture. Chrissy could see Beth and her other friends cheering and waving, too. She was a hit!

"I knew it," Robin said after Chrissy's second song elicited the same enthusiastic response. "They love you, Chrissy."

Chrissy put her arm around Robin and the applause increased. "They love *us*," she insisted. Then she turned slightly and gestured at Gary, Van, and Dave. The crowd cheered even louder. "They love *all* of us."

Then, as the applause began to die down, Chrissy walked back to Van's keyboard. "Play something slow and romantic, will you? You know, something that's just right to dance to."

Van grinned. "I know just what you're talking about, Chrissy." He started playing an instrumental version of Chrissy's favorite Angelina song, "I'm Your Girl." The rest of the band joined in, and Chrissy hopped down from the stage and approached Duncan. Taking off the hat, she settled it back on his head.

"Did you mean it?" he asked, his green eyes searching hers. "Really?"

Chrissy nodded. "I guess it's time we stopped fighting it."

Duncan chuckled as he gathered her close. "Won't our parents be thrilled?" he asked as they began swaying gently to the music.

Chrissy couldn't help grimacing. "That's something we'll just have to learn to live with, I guess."

"Mmmm," Duncan murmured against her ear. Then he said, "What is this song, anyway? I really like it."

"Don't you know?" Chrissy demanded, pulling back. "It's number one on the charts this week. It's called 'I'm Your Girl.' "

Duncan smiled. "And are you?"

Chrissy nodded, then leaned forward and covered his lips with a tender kiss. "I guess I always have been."